# BISHOP'S QUEEN

## ENDGAME TRILOGY

Katie Reus

Cover art: Jaycee of Sweet 'N Spicy Designs
Editor: Julia Ganis
Author website: https://www.katiereus.com

Bishop's Queen /Katie Reus. -- 1st ed.
KR Press, LLC

ISBN-13: 9781635561067
ISBN-10: 163556106X

*For Kaylea Cross, who is more like a sister than a friend.*

# Praise for the novels of Katie Reus

"Exciting in more ways than one, well-paced and smoothly written, I'd recommend *A Covert Affair* to any romantic suspense reader."
—Harlequin Junkie

"Sexy military romantic suspense." —USA Today

"I could not put this book down. . . . Let me be clear that I am not saying that this was a good book *for* a paranormal genre; it was an excellent romance read, *period.*" —All About Romance

"Reus strikes just the right balance of steamy sexual tension and nail-biting action. . . . This romantic thriller reliably hits every note that fans of the genre will expect." —*Publishers Weekly*

"Prepare yourself for the start of a great new series! . . . I'm excited about reading more about this great group of characters."
—Fresh Fiction

"Wow! This powerful, passionate hero sizzles with sheer deliciousness. I loved every sexy twist of this fun & exhilarating tale. Katie Reus delivers!" —Carolyn Crane, RITA award winning author

"A sexy, well-crafted paranormal romance that succeeds with smart characters and creative world building."—Kirkus Reviews

"*Mating Instinct*'s romance is taut and passionate . . . Katie Reus's newest installment in her Moon Shifter series will leave readers breathless!"
—Stephanie Tyler, *New York Times* bestselling author

"You'll fall in love with Katie's heroes."
—*New York Times* bestselling author, Kaylea Cross

"Both romantic and suspenseful, a fast-paced sexy book full of high stakes action." —Heroes and Heartbreakers

"Katie Reus pulls the reader into a story line of second chances, betrayal, and the truth about forgotten lives and hidden pasts."
—The Reading Café

"Nonstop action, a solid plot, good pacing, and riveting suspense."
—RT Book Reviews

"Enough sexual tension to set the pages on fire."
—*New York Times* bestselling author, Alexandra Ivy

"...a wild hot ride for readers. The story grabs you and doesn't let go."
—*New York Times* bestselling author, Cynthia Eden

"Has all the right ingredients: a hot couple, evil villains, and a killer action-filled plot. . . . [The] Moon Shifter series is what I call Grade-A entertainment!" —Joyfully Reviewed

"*Avenger's Heat* hits the ground running...This is a story of strength, of partnership and healing, and it does it brilliantly."
—Vampire Book Club

"*Mating Instinct* was a great read with complex characters, serious political issues and a world I am looking forward to coming back to."
—All Things Urban Fantasy

# CHAPTER ONE

Exhausted, Isla stepped into a local Miami restaurant owned by Viktor Ivanov, smiling politely at the maître d' as she shed her coat. The restaurant was inside a posh hotel so it was a mix of locals and tourists. "I believe my party is already here, Geno Conti."

"Of course, Ms. McDonald, this way."

As she followed after him, she gave a real smile, surprised to see Dominique Ivanov out with her husband, Viktor. The two people couldn't be more opposite, with Dominique a bright ray of sunshine, and definitely glowing now that she was pregnant.

As she stopped at the table, the maître d' stood off to the side, politely waiting for her as she hugged her friend.

"You're probably the most adorable pregnant woman I've ever seen. You're completely glowing." She was all belly and cuteness.

"This is true," Viktor said, also standing and giving her one of his rare smiles and a half hug.

For some reason Viktor had always been incredibly kind and warm with Isla. It probably had something to do with the fact that she was friends with Dominique, because he had a ruthless reputation with people who crossed him. Thankfully she'd never seen that side of him.

"You have to say that," Dominique said, grinning at her husband.

As Isla watched the two of them, an ache settled in her chest. Two months ago, she'd been in what she'd thought was the perfect relationship. She'd been so secure in what she'd had. But the bombing had changed everything. Her father was dead, and while her fiancé was alive, he might as well have died too. He'd coldly cut her out of his life as if she didn't exist after he'd been injured in the explosion. No amount of trying to see him had worked either.

And she had tried hard.

Even now, as she tried to work with his company on finishing the deal her father and Evan had started, she only dealt with Evan's assistant because he would not see her. It was so cruel, so unlike the man she'd loved.

It was as if she'd lost a limb, a part of herself. And she could admit that she was still floundering, trying to get used to this new reality two months later. Now she pasted on a smile for the world, refusing to let anyone see her pain. She was used to it. As the daughter of a highly functioning alcoholic, she knew how to put on her best smile and fake it.

"What are you doing here?" Dominique asked. "I mean, obviously you're here for dinner, but who are you meeting? Evan?" she asked hopefully.

The smile froze on her face. So much for faking it. "Ah...no."

Dominique blinked in surprise. "I...I saw him here earlier and I thought maybe you two..."

"Oh, no. I'm just here for business," she continued, not wanting to talk about Evan, and glad she hadn't bumped into him here. That would have been like taking a dagger to the heart.

"Well expect an invitation soon to a shower for this little guy." Dominique quickly changed the subject, thankfully.

"I will. I'll see you guys later."

"Thank you for waiting," she said to the maître d', who was still patiently standing there. He smiled politely and led her to a table in the back.

Geno Conti stood when he saw her, and went to pull her chair out but she waved him away. This was business, not a personal date.

As she set her purse and attaché case down, she ordered a sparkling water, putting Evan from her mind. "Sorry I'm running late. A meeting ran over."

"It's no problem, I know how it is. You don't want anything stronger than water?"

She shook her head. "I'm good." On occasion she drank—she made an exception for really good champagne—but she abstained at work functions. And she was always careful not to drink too much. It was just one of those things because of how she'd grown up. Her mother used to stash bottles—usually of vodka, because it was easier to hide the smell—all over the house to hide them from her father, sometimes in Isla's own room. But she shook the unhappy thought off.

"So, let's get started," she said, smiling at the man across from her. Her father had started a big business deal with Geno before he'd been killed, and Isla hoped to complete it.

There were a few different deals she was trying to close before she stepped back from the company. Her father's dream had never been her dream, but she would honor his legacy by taking care of the deals that had meant the most to him. Especially since they would be creating thousands of jobs as well. But once the deals were complete, she was letting people much more motivated than her take over. Unfortunately the process was taking longer than she had anticipated. Before the bombing she'd been a project manager in charge of various construction deals, and she'd been happy enough. Now, she ran the whole company and it was draining her soul.

"I'm ready if you are," he said, smiling in that charming way of his. With dark hair, dark eyes, a sharp jawline and a perfect olive complexion, he was definitely easy on the eyes.

Geno was always in the tabloids—being linked to various women, and never the same one twice. At first she'd been wary of doing business with him, but he had been nothing but professional, which was a relief. Especially since it wasn't always that way with the men she dealt with. While her father was alive and when she'd been linked to Evan Bishop, she'd been treated differently. She could see the stark difference and it was eye-opening. Not that she needed a male protector, but apparently she was seen as fair game to some people now. While it was revolting, it had helped her to weed out some people she'd been considering for senior management positions.

Banishing those thoughts, she leaned down and pulled out her tablet. She was glad they were in the back where they could get some business out of the way. She wished they'd been able to meet during normal hours, but between the two of them, they hadn't been able to carve out any free time. Even with Geno's playboy reputation, he was incredibly driven.

"I can think of worse ways to spend a Thursday night," Geno said two hours later as he pushed his after-dinner coffee to the side.

She smiled, laughing slightly. "Agreed." They'd gone over everything they needed to and they were on the same page. "So tomorrow night, you and me, the Sanderson gala. We'll corner Rodriguez and see if we can lock this thing down."

"Works for me."

At that moment, the maître d' stopped at their table. "Mr. Ivanov wanted me to let you know that dinner is on the house."

"Oh no, that's not necessary. Just charge it to my business account," Isla said.

He shook his head. "Mr. Ivanov's orders."

At that moment she knew it was pointless to argue. "Please thank him for me, then." She planned to tell him that herself on the way out if he was still here.

He nodded politely and then left as quietly as he'd arrived.

"I didn't realize you knew Ivanov." Geno's surprise was clear.

She nodded. "Yes, I'm friends with his wife."

"Ah. I hear they're expecting."

"Yes, I'm very happy for both of them... Well, I guess we're done here. I can meet you at the gala or at my office at the end of the day. I won't be going home first."

He set his napkin on the table. "I'll pick you up at work."

Standing, she gathered her things. "Sounds good." This deal was so close to being complete she could almost taste it. *You're almost there,* she reminded herself. She simply needed all this stuff behind her so she could find her own two feet and make a life for herself—not live a dream that had been her father's. She'd already had one foot out the door of the business before her father had died. But now? She felt stuck.

When Geno was stopped by an associate of his, she made a quick escape, glad to be able to get out of there and head home. Lately she felt as if she was on autopilot, and it wasn't a mystery as to why. She missed Evan. Deeply. Without him in her life, everything felt empty.

*Ugh.* She had to stop thinking about him.

As Isla waited at the valet, she checked her cell phone, not surprised to see multiple texts from her mother, texts from work, and a handful from a few friends. However, she was surprised to see one from Evie Bishop—Evan's younger sister. A cool breeze reminding her that fall was moving in fast this year rolled over her as she pulled up Evie's text message first.

*I'm going to the gala tomorrow, will I see you there?*

Of course Evie would be there. She was a Bishop, and now that she had moved back to town she went to plenty of events with her new husband, Dylan Blackwood. The man owned half the city. Sometimes Isla felt a little odd staying in touch with Evie since they'd almost become sisters-in-law, but Evie had made it clear she thought Evan was a dumbass for his behavior. Something she'd told Isla on multiple occasions.

*I'll be there for work,* she texted back. *And I know you're going only under duress,* she added. Because Evie hated these kinds of things.

Evie responded with a bunch of laughing emojis and *#truth,* which just made Isla laugh.

As she started to scan the rest of her messages, an SUV with dark-tinted windows jerked to a halt underneath the overhang. One of the valet drivers stepped out from behind the stand where he was talking with a coworker when the door to the SUV flew open and a masked man jumped out.

Her heart jumped in her throat as the guy lunged for her, ripping her attaché case from her hand.

Screaming, she swung out with her bag, barely grazing his shoulder. She saw the fist coming and ducked, but he slammed into her, sending her flying backward.

Her heel caught on a stone, snapping as she rolled her ankle and landed on her butt.

"Hey!" Multiple male voices shouted, their footsteps pounding as they came running.

But her attacker had already jumped back into the vehicle. Tires squealed as he tore off into the night.

She'd barely pushed upright when a man wearing a valet uniform was crouching in front of her. His eyes were wide as he held out a hand to her. "Are you okay?"

Behind him, another employee was already talking into a phone, with what sounded like the police.

Trembling, she nodded and winced as she stood. She'd landed on her butt hard. "He took my bag."

"The police will be on their way soon," he said. "Why don't you step inside the hotel? We've got a private place you can sit."

Still shaking, she nodded and followed after him. Everything had happened so fast, she hadn't been ready for it. But who was actually ready to be mugged? She was just glad that she had taken her laptop out earlier. There had been some paperwork in there but nothing confidential. Just little notes she'd made.

For the briefest moment, she had the urge to call Evan. It would be pointless of course, but she'd gotten so used to him having her back.

Not tonight. Never again.

# CHAPTER TWO

Evan stripped off his boxing gloves and tossed them onto the workbench in his private gym. He owned the penthouse of a Miami condo downtown and he'd had a personal gym built in it, even before his accident.

Before the bombing had blown everything to hell.

Now he was grateful for it. He didn't have to deal with people staring at him if he wanted to work out without a shirt on.

The blast had scorched his neck, down his right arm and part of his chest. His scars looked like a mashing of red, twisting ropes, creating a macabre display all over his right side. Part of his face had suffered as well, but he'd since grown a beard and it covered most of his face. According to his mother, he was trying to hide away from the world and the beard was a big fat symbol of that.

She was probably right. No, she was definitely right. But he didn't care.

He grabbed a towel and glanced at his cell phone. He was surprised to see a call from Viktor Ivanov. They'd done some deals together, but before seven in the morning was fairly early to be calling and they didn't have a current project in the works. And they weren't friends. Curious, he called back.

"Bishop," Ivanov said upon greeting. "Thank you for returning my call."

"Is everything okay?"

"I do not know. Your fiancée— Ah, former fiancée, was at my restaurant last night. She was mugged when leaving. It was done very quickly, professionally. They took her work briefcase."

Shock punched through him. "Is Isla okay?" he rasped out. If this had happened two months ago, he would've already known. She would have woken up in bed with him this morning.

"I believe she is fine. A little sore and maybe bruised. The man pushed her down but that was the basic extent of it."

Evan sucked in a sharp breath. Someone had laid hands on Isla? A murderous rage popped through him, sharp and violent in its intensity, knocking him off-kilter.

"I have watched the video footage, and he grazed her shoulder because she was quick-thinking enough to move back. I don't like that this happened on my property, however. I don't like that it happened at all, especially to someone as sweet as her. I know you two are not... Ah—" Ivanov cleared his throat awkwardly. "Anyway, Dominique thought I should tell you, regardless."

If the situation had been any different, Evan might have snorted or laughed. Viktor Ivanov had a ruthless reputation but he did whatever his wife wanted. "Thank you for telling me. What did the police say?"

"They will be looking into it, but there was something obscuring the license plate, and the man had on a mask."

Evan frowned, a lead ball settling in his gut. "Was she targeted specifically?"

"It looks very specific to me. The police wanted to know about her different business deals, and considering what happened to her father and you, I hope they take this seriously."

"Thank you."

They made no small talk after that, just quickly disengaged, something Evan was grateful for. On the best of days, he had no energy for small talk and this was not a good day. Not now that he knew Isla had been mugged.

As he set his phone down he grabbed another towel and rubbed it over his head. He needed to shower and he had to fight the deeply instinctive urge to rush right over to Isla's condo. She wasn't his. And never would be again. He'd made sure of it.

He wasn't going to tie her to a broken man—not when it was his fault her father was dead.

When talking to Ivanov it hadn't occurred to him to question who had been with Isla at the restaurant, so he quickly texted the question. He wanted to know if there had been another witness.

A moment later, he found himself glaring at his cell phone screen. Isla had been with Geno Conti. A pretty boy who slept with any willing woman, it seemed. He'd heard from a source that Conti and Isla were working on a deal together, but this could have just as easily been a date.

Annoyed, he scrubbed a hand over his face and left his gym. Once he was in the shower, letting the hot jets blast over him, he found himself consumed with thoughts of Isla.

As always.

He used to love running his hands through her thick, auburn tresses—while they'd showered together. Hell, they'd spent every free second they'd had together. He would sneak away for lunches even though he should have been working, usually meeting her at one of the local food trucks. He would have done anything for just a few extra minutes a day with her.

He'd even taken up running so he'd get to spend more time in the mornings with her—and he'd found that he enjoyed it. Isla had always pretended not to be competitive, but then at the end of their runs she would sprint ahead and pump her fists in the air like Rocky.

Then she would laugh, the most beautiful sound in the world, her bright green eyes sparkling as she did—

*No.* He had to stop thinking about her. That was impossible, however, because when he closed his eyes, he saw her. He had every curve, every line of her body memorized, including the way her full breasts felt in his palms as he cupped them, teased them.

She was petite, barely hitting five feet two, and she'd fit perfectly against him in every way.

When he realized he was stroking himself to thoughts of her, he stopped, grinding his teeth together. *No.*

He turned the shower to cold and quickly finished, hurrying to the office in his condo. He wasn't good company today and didn't think he would make it to the main office of Bishop Enterprises. The building itself had been completely renovated since the bombing and there hadn't been any real structural damage. It was as if it had never happened. But nothing could erase the past.

Shaking those thoughts off, he focused on the day at hand. He had no meetings that he couldn't simply Skype. And his assistant Ricardo was more than capable of dealing with any issues.

He flipped on two of his televisions, watching the stocks in the background as he pulled up one of his many email accounts.

He frowned as an image of Isla and Geno flashed onscreen, clearly taken with someone's cell phone. Stupid gossip. That was the problem with living in Miami—celebrities were everywhere, and Isla's family was well-known and wealthy. But Conti was the real reason they were on the news. Gossip rags loved anything to do with troublemaker Conti. Though in the past year Evan didn't remember reading anything negative about the man. Apparently he was cleaning up his act.

His annoyance surging, Evan changed the channel but found himself doing an online search.

When he saw another story about Isla and Conti with the writer speculating if the two were now an item, he resisted the urge to smash his laptop. Feeling his mood grow darker, he turned it off.

But he couldn't get the image of Isla smiling at Conti out of his head no matter how hard he tried. At twenty-eight, she was a decade younger than Evan, something that had never mattered between them. But seeing that picture with Conti, a man the same age as her who looked as if he fit perfectly with her? Yep, he definitely needed to hit something.

# CHAPTER THREE

Isla had just stepped out of her private executive bathroom when she heard a knock on her office door. She was fairly certain she knew who it was. "Come in."

"Hey, it's just me." Madeleine, one of her senior-level executives—who she was seriously considering moving up to the CFO position—stepped in. Her brown hair was pulled back into a twist and she was wearing her standard pantsuit.

"Hey." She smiled at the other woman. "Mind helping me with the zipper?" Her dress was a mix of sparkles and lace, with a scalloped V-neck and delicate flutter sleeves.

Madeleine let out a low whistle. "Your dress is gorgeous. And so are you. Now I'm almost jealous I'm not going tonight."

Isla snorted and turned around, lifting her hair so Madeleine could pull the zipper up the rest of the way. Months ago she would have been excited to go to a big gala because she would have had Evan by her side. Now? She'd rather be at home, away from all people. Healthy? Nope. But it was the truth. Madeleine, however, had no interest in stuff like this. "You are such a liar. You're going to go home to Alena and the two of you are going to enjoy an amazing night, not wearing stupid heels and making pointless chitchat with tons of strangers."

"Aren't you just a ray of sunshine? And you're also completely correct. I wouldn't mind getting dressed up though. It feels like it's been forever since Alena and I have gone on a date."

"I have two extra tickets to the Cirque show. It's actually why I called you up here. I was going to see if you wanted them. It's for next weekend, so it's a little last minute. One of the vendors gave them to me." And since she and Evan had gone in the past, it made her feel crappy to go without him. Which was beyond stupid, but there it was.

She was currently at the stage where she was avoiding many of the places she'd gone with Evan, so that covered a whole lot of the city. Eventually she would get out of this funk but it wasn't going to be today. And she was pragmatic enough to realize that. So she was embracing being in this ostrich mode where she simply buried her head in the sand regarding all things Evan.

"Are you serious?" Madeleine said.

She strode to her desk and pulled out the tickets. "They're actual physical tickets. How cute is that?" she said, handing them over. Almost everything was electronic now but her vendor was kind of old-school.

"Thank you. Alena was talking about this weeks ago but it was already sold out."

"I'm glad you'll be able to enjoy them. So is there anything new to report other than the email recap you sent?"

"Nothing other than I let Rodney Wood go today. I waited until the end of the day and called him in. We're going to give him a severance." Her tone was dry because she didn't think Rodney deserved one.

Isla nodded, glad that was one more thing taken care of. Rodney had been with the company a decade and she wasn't sure how he'd slipped through the cracks. The man was a mediocre engineer whose credentials weren't nearly as impressive as he'd led the company to believe. Top that off with atrocious soft skills and he'd been seriously harming his division, creating a toxic atmosphere. She wanted to grow her father's business—well, her business, technically—not stifle true talent. She'd discovered that they'd already lost a few people because of Rodney after she reviewed some of the exit interviews, and she wasn't going to lose any more good people because of a bad apple. "Thanks for handling that."

"Just doing my job."

"Well, you are doing a damn good job." Isla almost told Madeleine that she wanted to talk to her about the CFO position, but held back. She wasn't ready to finalize anything yet. Soon though.

"So...I know this is not work-related and kind of gossipy," Madeleine said, "but I saw the news today."

She stared blankly at Madeleine. "About the upcoming deal?" She'd scanned online this morning, but hadn't seen anything interesting.

"No. About you and Geno Conti...in the gossip section. I was wondering if you guys were dating?"

She snorted, some of the tension inside her easing. As long as there wasn't any speculation about any of her upcoming deals—that she desperately wanted to wrap up—

she didn't care. "There's not enough money in the world."

Madeleine let out a startled laugh. "He is pretty though."

"True enough. And he's a hell of a lot smarter than people give him credit for. Most people assume he got his job because of his father, and I know there is a lot of truth in that. But he's kind of a math nerd if you can believe it, and he's fantastic with people in a way that his brother and father aren't. He's a good asset." And she had a feeling his family didn't appreciate it, probably because of the reputation Geno had created for himself.

Madeleine lifted an eyebrow. "Thinking of poaching him from his dad?"

Isla grinned, lifting a shoulder. "Nah. So what did the gossip column say, anyway?"

"Nothing really. There was just a picture of you two at a restaurant, and the writer was speculating whether you'd finally moved on from—" Madeleine's eyes widened and she cleared her throat. "Anyway, it was just trash with nothing to back it up."

Isla ignored the near comment on Evan, burying thoughts of him down deep. They had no place in her head. Not tonight, anyway. "Thank you for letting me know about it. Seriously. If you see anything else like that, let me know." Isla was bad about checking stuff online, especially lately. She'd been so consumed with her father's projects. Heck, she couldn't even remember the last time she'd checked her only social media account. It was too much of a time suck and she had far too much

BISIIOP'S QUEEN | 25

to do lately. And if she was being completely honest with herself, she didn't want to stumble across anything that might mention Evan.

"Will do. And I know tonight is work, but I hope you have fun. You deserve it."

She doubted she'd have fun for a long time yet, but she kept that negativity to herself. "Thanks. I'm hoping to get the ball rolling with Sara Rodriguez." If she and Geno could just get Rodriguez to sign off on a few things, they'd be that much closer to wrapping up this business and Isla could focus on other projects.

"Just let me know if you need anything on my end."

"I will."

Now she just had to get through the rest of the night. One thing she was grateful for: it was almost guaranteed Evan wouldn't be at the gala. He'd given up on all social events lately. The reasoning for it broke her heart, but the man himself had broken it more.

She was glad not to have to worry about seeing him tonight.

\* \* \*

Since Geno had run behind with some of his meetings, Isla had agreed to meet him at the gala and was grateful for it. Her hired car pulled up front where photographers were already waiting. She definitely wasn't famous enough to warrant tons of pictures, but she was sure they would snap a few of her. If only because she was the daughter of a former beauty queen and a man who had recently been killed in a bombing that had rocked the city.

She mentally prepped herself as the door was opened for her. Lifting up the hem of her long dress slightly to avoid snagging it on her heels, she stepped out and plastered on a smile. She'd learned that it was much better to be always smiling than to have no facial expressions. Because if someone caught you in the picture looking like you were frowning, people speculated that a million different things were wrong. It was obnoxious. But it was just the way it was. As she moved forward, she ignored the twinge of discomfort from her mugging. She knew it could have been a lot worse than some uncomfortable soreness and she was grateful for that.

To her surprise Geno stepped out of the car right behind hers.

Laughing lightly, she waited until he joined her. "That's some great timing," she said as they headed up the red carpet together, ignoring the flash of cameras—and people calling out Geno's name.

"You look fantastic." His smile was easy and affable.

"You look pretty good yourself."

"I'm sure you saw the garbage article about us," he said, taking her elbow as they moved up the stairs leading to the door.

"Yes. Hopefully it won't have a dampening effect on your social life," she teased. He really was easy to be around.

He simply snorted and held out their invitations as they reached the door. "There are far worse things than people thinking you and I are dating."

She gave a forced laugh because she wasn't sure how to respond.

"Can I be blunt?" he asked as they stepped past the entrance.

People were everywhere, many faces she recognized. She waved at a woman she'd gone to college with, but kept up with the flow of people as she and Geno made their way to the ballroom entrance. So far it didn't seem to be crushing, just a steady flow of women and men in elegant dresses and tuxes. "Sure."

"Would you like to go on a date with me after this deal is closed?"

She froze and stared at him, trying to find her voice—trying to figure out how to politely reject him. She wasn't sure what her expression looked like but he actually winced.

"All right, then. I've got my answer." Laughter filled his voice, thankfully. "You're hell on my ego—which is probably good," he continued. "At least according to my sister. She said I need to be knocked down a few pegs. Mission accomplished."

Despite the awkwardness, Isla found herself laughing out loud at his bluntness. "You took me off guard. The answer is definitely no, but—"

He laughed again, the sound drawing looks from a few people around them. "You really don't hold back. I think that's why I find you so refreshing. And I've got to say Evan Bishop is a dumbass."

"Hey," she snapped. Even if she was angry at Evan, she didn't want anyone else talking like that about him. It made her claws come out—and that surprised her.

Still holding on to her elbow, he continued guiding them through the throng of people. "I like the guy, a lot. I'm just saying he's a dumbass for letting you go. That's it."

Despite herself, her mouth curved up into a smile. "Sometimes you're nothing like I expected... And others, a little bit what I expected." It was clear he was a playboy, but the man was a hell of a lot smarter than people gave him credit for. She'd learned that in the short time they'd been working together. Now she understood why her father had teamed up with him to close this deal instead of Geno's father or brother. The man was easy to work with and her father had likely figured that his charm would go a long way in closing things with Sara Rodriguez.

He full-on grinned and she suppressed a laugh when a nearby woman did a double take, staring at him. "Yeah, I get that a lot. People are always surprised to find out I'm not just a pretty face." Again with that charming smile.

She rolled her eyes and started to tell him that they needed to find Sara Rodriguez when they very nearly ran into Evie Bishop and Dylan Blackwood. Well, she guessed it was Evie Blackwood now. Still, she would always think of Evie as a Bishop.

"Isla." Evie stepped forward and pulled her into a tight hug. "You are absolutely stunning. I don't even want to stand next to you, you're so gorgeous."

Isla made a scoffing sound, even as her cheeks flushed. Evie was always so nice and Isla never knew what was going to come out of the woman's mouth. She'd been looking forward to getting Evie as a sister-in-law, to gaining all of the Bishops as family because they were just so wonderful. "You're out of your mind."

Dylan stepped up and gave her a quick hug, his smile genuine. None of the brooding from him she'd seen for the few months that he and Evie had been broken up. Now he just looked...happy. Settled. And the two of them deserved it.

"You look incredible," she added to Evie, because it was the truth. Though Isla was pretty sure everything looked good on her. Her long, black, one-shoulder gown was slightly ruched around her middle, but other than that it was simple and shimmery and fit Evie like it had been custom tailored for her. Which it probably had been. "I hope to see your parents here tonight too. Your mom sent me a text letting me know she would be here." Even with everything that had happened with Evan, she simply couldn't cut his parents out of her life. They'd been a lifeline as the three of them had been holed up in the hospital waiting for news on Evan. Even though he'd cut Isla out of his life, she still loved his parents, and they her.

"Oh, they're around here somewhere. Ah, and here's Evan." Evie motioned over Isla's shoulder.

Ice coated her veins as Evie's words sank in. He couldn't be here. No. *No, no, no.* He'd been avoiding events since he'd gotten out of the hospital, and avoiding her at every turn. But tonight, when she wasn't prepared, he showed up?

*Come on!* she mentally shouted at the universe. *Cut me some slack.*

Even as she felt that ice spread outward at a slow crawl, she kept a pleasant smile plastered on her face and found herself leaning a little closer to Geno, who still held on to her elbow. If she was being honest, she was grateful for Geno's presence.

At one time she'd wanted nothing more than to see Evan, to demand answers, but she wasn't in the right mental headspace tonight. She felt like she was free-falling, hurtling through the air with the ground rushing up at her. And now she had to face the man who'd broken her heart with absolutely no warning. The universe was clearly pissed at her for something.

As she turned to greet Evan, it was like a sucker punch to the chest. He looked savagely beautiful— though that was probably the wrong word, but savage definitely fit. He'd grown a beard and she could see the fading redness of the scars on the left side of his face where the dark hair hadn't quite covered it. The tight-looking, reddish scars extended down to his neck and beyond, but the rest was covered by his tux. She knew that eventually the scars would fade to white, but it was far too soon for that.

She had the insane urge to reach up and touch him, to embrace him. To freaking scream at him and ask him why he'd cut her out of her life as if she was nothing. *Oh, no.* She shoved back her rage. She'd spent a lifetime smiling through her pain and worry where her mom was concerned. She could deal with seeing her ex for a few minutes and make inane small talk, even if she was quietly dying inside.

"Isla, Geno, nice to see you both." Evan's words weren't exactly icy, but they weren't friendly either.

It was like being slapped in the face with cold water. He spoke to her as if they'd never made love in every room of his home—and hers. As if they hadn't actually been engaged. As if they were mere strangers being painfully polite because they had to be.

Turned out she was wrong. She most definitely could not keep up the pretense of being friendly to the man who'd broken her heart. Not for much longer, anyway.

Geno stuck his hand out and for a moment Isla wasn't certain Evan would take it. He was almost always perfectly polite, even if he was cold to people, but he was looking at Geno as if he wanted to rip his head off. His sharp blue eyes narrowed ever so slightly, a dark glint in them.

She frowned, looking between the two of them. There was no way he was jealous. Not when he'd been the one to cut her out of his life.

After an uncomfortable pause, he shook Geno's hand. "Nice to see you."

Geno didn't let go and neither did Evan, both of them doing some weird kind of hard grip as they stared at each other. What the hell was going on? She looked over at Evie, who was watching them in fascination, her eyes gleaming in...amusement?

Isla cleared her throat. She didn't have time for whatever garbage this was. "Well, we need to make some rounds."

When neither of them moved, Isla wrapped her fingers around Geno's upper arm. "I see Rodriguez," she said.

He glanced at her in surprise, letting go of Evan's hand.

She murmured polite nothings as she practically dragged Geno away, letting the throng of people swallow them up. She shoved back the hurt bubbling up inside that Evan hadn't said one personal thing, had barely tried to be polite, and had basically had a strange sort of pissing contest with Geno.

As they moved their way through the tables, disappearing into the crowd, Geno looked around. "Where is she?"

"I lied. You two looked like you needed to be separated."

He looked startled then laughed.

And she found herself laughing as well, though it surprised her. God, it felt good to actually let loose, to not be this tight ball of tense energy all the time. And even if it was just for one night, she was going to at least try to enjoy herself since she had to be here anyway. Because screw Evan Bishop. She might be dying inside, but that didn't mean she had to be crappy company for the man she was doing business with tonight. Geno had showed up here ready to get things done and he deserved a partner who was ready to work too—not wallow in self-pity.

"We'll find her soon."

"Would you like some champagne?"

"I'm okay. Sparkling water will be fine."

"All right, then. Let's get some drinks and find Rodriguez."

As they mingled, making their way toward one of the drink areas, she forced herself not to turn and look back in the direction they'd left Evan. Even if she swore she could feel his eyes drilling into her back.

That was just her imagination, however. It had to be.

CHAPTER FOUR

Isla stepped out of the huge ladies' room, glad to be away from all of the chattering and people. She and Geno had done what they'd come to do, and though she knew she would have to stick around for another half hour and make small talk, she was ready to go. Months ago, she would have been in her element. So many of her family's friends and acquaintances were here and she loved catching up with people. She was a social butterfly and normally loved stuff like this.

But two months ago, she would have been with Evan, so tonight would have been fun and would have ended with a couple bouts of satisfying, sweaty sex. Right now, she felt as if she was on autopilot, just going through the motions. Though she was pretty sure she'd stayed upbeat with Geno and Sara Rodriguez.

Seeing Evan had thrown her off-balance. No use denying it.

As she rounded the corner, the noise and music grew louder— She jerked to a halt to stop from running into Evan. It was as if her mind had conjured him up. Or maybe the universe was still screwing with her. *Ugh.*

He was alone, looking sexy in his custom tux, and she wanted to drink in every inch of him. But he might as well be a stranger.

She smiled politely, unsure what to say as she started to step around him. She absolutely could not do bullshit small talk with this man. This man who had seen every inch of her naked, who had eaten food off her body, given her far too many orgasms to count, and asked her to be his *wife*. Nope. If she started talking to him, she was likely to unleash all the hurt and anger buried inside. And once she started, she wouldn't stop. Making a public scene was not something she'd ever done, nor intended to do. But her emotions were riding high tonight.

"You and Geno?" His voice was a rough growl as he spoke.

She jerked to a halt at the very fact that he was talking to her. It took a moment for his angry words to register. "What?"

His stare was laser-hot. "Are you seeing Geno Conti?"

She blinked again. "We're here on business. Something I'm pretty sure you're already aware of." Unless he was seriously out of touch with everything, and Evan always had a pulse on everything around Miami.

"I saw the article online."

"And you believe everything you read online now?" She couldn't believe they were even having this conversation. He owed her so much more than this, owed her an explanation and an apology, and this was all he had to say? Oh, her anger spiked now, sharp and hot, needling away at her insides.

"Stay away from him."

Her spine straightened. "Excuse me?"

"Don't fuck him."

Her eyes widened as she stared at him in pure shock. To be fair, he looked a little shocked by his own words. Still, he couldn't seriously be telling her who she could or couldn't sleep with. She had so many responses, but none of them came out as she stared at this arrogant, domineering man she'd fallen for over a year ago. Right about now she wanted to smack that look right off his face.

"I will sleep with whoever I want, wherever I want— as many times as I want. And in as many different positions as I want." She stepped around him then, hurt and fury stabbing her with sharp needles, ignoring his growl of protest. There was no way she was sleeping with Geno, but Evan didn't get to tell her what to do. He'd lost the right to even call her a friend.

Forget waiting half an hour. She was leaving now. She was hanging on by a thread and Evan had just pushed her to the brink. She was going to go home and get in her pajamas.

And probably eat a pint of ice cream.

Because if she stayed any longer, she was going to completely lose it and then she'd end up in the gossip section of multiple online outlets tomorrow. *Nope, nope, nope.*

\* \* \*

On the couch in her condo living room as she looked out over brightly lit downtown Miami, Isla paused at a consistent knocking sound.

No one should be at her door because security hadn't announced any visitors. Not to mention it was midnight. Though technically it could be one of her neighbors. Annoyed, she pulled up her security camera from her phone and froze when she saw Evan on the screen, knocking on her door. She'd left him at the gala nearly an hour ago. *What the hell?*

Ugh, he'd been here so many times in the past, security had probably just waved him on through.

Annoyed beyond reason and ready to light into him, she stalked to the front door and jerked it open. "Excuse me? Can I help you?"

He was still in his tux, his tie gone and his shirt rumpled. He stalked right past her as if he had every right to.

"Oh my God. What the hell is wrong with you? You can't just barge in here."

She stared at his very sexy backside as he stopped in the foyer and swiveled to face her, looking as if he'd collected himself somewhat. But he still hadn't said a word. That was when it registered why he was here. *Oh no.* The anger was back, all those spikes of fury lashing out against her senses.

"You think Geno is here, don't you?" When he didn't deny it, she stared at him for a long moment. "My only date tonight is Ben and Jerry. I'm alone. Not that it's any of your business. Geno and I are working on a business deal. People of the opposite sex can indeed do business together and have it just be business." *Despite what some morons might think.*

He rubbed a hand over his dark hair, looking almost lost. "I shouldn't have come over here."

"No kidding. I'm curious though—what would you have done if he *had* been in my bed?"

Fire shot through his eyes. "I don't even want to think about what I would have done."

"What's wrong with you?" she demanded, completely at the end of her rope with him. "*You* ended things with me, and didn't even have the balls to do it to my face." Hell, they'd been planning to move in together before they got married. Her entire condo had been packed up and ready to be moved into his place. But that had never happened so she'd had to unpack and put everything back up. She still had a few boxes lying around that she hadn't managed to unload because it had been too depressing.

Now was the time for this, she realized. She finally had Evan in front of her and she couldn't stop the deluge of things she'd been desperate to say to him. Even if she should hold back, there was no stopping her now.

In her bare feet and navy blue pajamas covered in white stars that her mother had given her, she stepped forward, thrusting her index finger at him. "I have some things I want to say to you, and you are going to listen."

He didn't move, just watched her, his blue eyes focused on her.

"The fact that you're here right now, the fact you're telling me to basically stay away from Geno, is seriously messed up. You cut me out of your life in a way I wouldn't even do to an enemy." That wasn't true. "Scratch that—you cut me out of your life the way I would do to an enemy. What you did was brutal, and *cruel.*"

Now that she was on a roll, there was no stopping.

"My father had just died. And I understand you were in the hospital and in pain. Guess what, I was in pain too. I was hurting with loss, for my father, and for you. We were engaged. We loved each other. But you treated me like a stranger. What you did was beyond mean. It was unforgivable. Something I literally never could have imagined happening." Her breaths were coming in raspy now as she balled her fists at her side, resisting the urge to punch him. "You ripped my *heart* out!"

He opened his mouth to respond but she shook her head.

"No. Stay there. I have something for you." Hurt and anger swirled inside her as she hurried into her bedroom and grabbed the little jewelry box she'd been foolishly holding on to the last couple months.

He'd never asked for the engagement ring back, and she'd been planning to give it to him. But she'd been holding on to the thing as a sort of security blanket. If she still had this ring, then they weren't really broken up. He hadn't *really* savagely cut her out of his life. Except he had. It was time for her to get over him and move on, no matter how hard it was or how much it hurt.

In a full rage now, she stopped back in the foyer where he was still standing, hands shoved in his pockets. She held out the box, and when he slowly reached out a hand, she slammed it into his palm. "I should have given this back to you a long time ago. Stay out of my life. I already told you, I'll date or sleep with whoever I want. You made your feelings about me very clear. You made it really clear that you didn't think I could handle you being injured! As if you thought I would run away at the first sign of things getting difficult. Which made me realize you didn't know me at all. That you had absolutely no faith in *us*."

His expression was tortured. "Isla—"

"No. You lost the right to try and explain long ago, and I don't want to hear a thing you have to say at this point. I am absolutely done with you, Evan Bishop. Do you understand that? Do not come back over to my house. We're done." She opened the door, grabbed him by the upper arm and propelled him out.

He was strong enough that he didn't have to move if he didn't want to, but he let her push him along even though it was clear he wanted to say something.

She couldn't stand hearing anything from him right now. No platitudes, no stupid apologies, nothing. Because if he said anything remotely apologetic, she was going to burst into tears. She'd cried enough for Evan. And he'd lost the right to talk to her now. She'd waited in that hospital for weeks, desperate to see him, for him to wake up from that coma. Then she'd been so sure the doctor was wrong and that Evan hadn't ordered her barred from his room. The very thought had been inconceivable.

Screw him and all the pain he'd caused her. The pain he was still causing her.

Surprising herself, she slammed the door in his face, and slid the lock into place. Then she collapsed against it and didn't fight the tears any longer, letting them stream down her face as her entire body shook. They were truly and utterly done, even if it felt like she'd just ripped her own skin off.

She'd known it, but tonight sealed the lid of the coffin shut on their relationship.

She and Evan were over, and she had to find a way to live with that.

CHAPTER FIVE

The next morning Evan stepped out of the condo across the hallway at the same time Isla did. Because he *might* have been watching through the peephole. Yep, this was what he'd been reduced to. All because of stupid life choices—and the fact that he was a damn coward. But he'd had a few hours of sleep and he knew what he needed to do. He had to make things right with her. The words she'd hurled at him last night had struck home. Hard. Because they'd been true.

She stared at him in confusion as she locked her door behind her. "What are you doing here?"

He drank in the sight of her, thirsty for her, hungry for her. Desperate to hold her again. He wasn't sure how he'd lived two months without her. Hell, he still had the letter she'd given him a month ago, telling him she'd always love him, be there for him—for some reason he couldn't toss it. When she'd given him back her engagement ring last night, everything had seemed so final. Which was his fault.

And the words she'd thrown at him had been one hundred percent true. What he'd done was beyond forgivable but he had to try and make things right. He knew she would never be with him again, but he didn't want to live in a world where Isla McDonald hated him so much. He needed...to at least be her friend. If she'd let him. She didn't deserve what he'd done to her, the way he'd cut her out of his life. He wanted more, but he was a realist. Now even more so than two months ago.

"I'm renting this place from Blackwood." He'd called the man after she'd kicked him out and asked to use the place indefinitely. Since Blackwood was married to Evan's sister, he hadn't given him any grief for calling so late.

As he stood with her, he tried not to do a visual sweep of her, though it was impossible. He had every curve and line of her body memorized—he'd thought about her endlessly while lying in that hospital bed. As he'd stared at the ceiling tiles, having memorized each crack or uneven placement, his thoughts had been consumed with Isla. He still loved her, had never stopped. But he'd had to let her go.

She had on regular running gear and he couldn't see any bruises from her mugging. According to Viktor she'd been shoved to the ground so she likely wouldn't have any visible bruises anyway. She seemed to be moving fine, just as she had last night. Watching her, it hit him again that she'd definitely lost weight. She didn't look frail, exactly, but she clearly wasn't taking care of herself. Damn it, he hated himself for being the cause of this.

"You look thinner," he blurted out, then inwardly cursed at the stony look she gave him.

She turned on her heel and started down the hallway.

"I'm sorry, that's not what I meant."

She simply snorted, doing a very good job of ignoring him as she strode toward the elevators. He followed. As they reached the mirrored doors, he studiously avoided looking at his reflection. He'd worn a long-sleeve shirt that covered up most of his scars but some were still visible along his neck and on the left side of his face. He was still getting used to the "new" him and though he hated the way his thoughts traveled, he wondered what Isla thought of him.

Last night at the gala she hadn't looked at him with disgust, like he'd feared, but with shock. Then she'd covered that up with a neutral mask of polite civility. And when she'd grasped onto Conti's arm, basically dragging the man away, he'd had to hold on to the last shred of control he had and force himself not to stalk after the two of them. The only reason he hadn't was because Evie had punched him in the shoulder and told him to stop being a dick. Even so, he still hadn't been unable to stop himself from hunting Isla down later—and acting like a complete jackass. When she'd told him that she'd sleep with whoever she wanted, whenever she wanted...

He rolled his shoulders. He couldn't go down that road either. *Keep it together,* he ordered himself.

"I'm sorry about a lot of things," he said quietly as they stepped into the elevator. He was surprised she was even listening to him so he took the opportunity to get all this out.

Her head tilted to the side slightly as she pressed the button for the ground floor, as if she was waiting for him to speak.

"I'm sorry for what I did. Everything you said last night, it hit home. You are a hundred percent right. There's no excuse for the way I handled things. I felt like a monster."

Hell, he still did. He barely recognized himself when he looked in the mirror.

"The thought of seeing you, of seeing pity on your face, was too much. So I acted like a coward. I... There's no excuse for what I did though. I know I hurt you and I'm sorry." God, so damn sorry. There was more than just the physicality of it all—though he hadn't been willing to saddle her with what he'd become. It was his fault her father had gotten killed—the security at Evan's building had been breached and that was on him. It had been his responsibility. He didn't deserve her, didn't deserve to be happy. He'd taken so much from her, and then the thought of her settling for him out of a sense of duty? No.

She remained silent, her jaw tight as she stared straight ahead. She'd never given him the silent treatment before and he didn't like it. At all.

But he also deserved it after basically doing the same thing to her. "I know I don't deserve your forgiveness. But I'm asking for it. I wish I knew how to make things right," he whispered.

The tightness in her shoulders lessened, but she still didn't respond as they stepped out of the elevators. He was ready to climb the damn walls with her ignoring him for two minutes and...he was beyond an asshole. God, when he thought about her in that waiting room at the hospital, just wanting news about him. To see him. Be there for him. And then he wouldn't let her back to see him... Yep, asshole.

When he'd seen her last night, looking thinner and watching him as if he was a stranger, the gravity of everything had hit home. He'd hurt her in a way he'd never imagined. Hell, he'd made a promise to not only not hurt her, but to take care of her, to love her. Instead? He'd screwed up. Beyond, even.

"You're going running?" he asked, then cursed himself again. He was Captain Obvious over here today. She had her armband on and her earbuds dangling from her shirt.

Lifting an eyebrow, she gave him a sideways look that said *No shit, Sherlock.*

"Can I run with you?" he asked.

She simply shrugged. "It's a free country."

All right, then. She wasn't cursing him out or yelling at him. He would take it. Then she put her earbuds in, shutting him out, but he didn't care as they stepped out into the morning sunlight. He breathed in the fresh, salt-tinged air, enjoying being next to Isla again. Even if she hated him.

Once upon a time, they'd always gone running together. It had been one of the many things they used to do as a couple. He missed the fresh air, missed this.

*Missed Isla.*

She was silent as they ran, but he didn't mind. They'd run in silence many times, just enjoying the city as it woke up. At a little after seven on a Saturday, he wasn't surprised that not many places were bustling. After about three miles, he knew where she was going before she even made the right turn at the next street.

One of the few places that would have a lot of activity was a farmer's market in a nearby neighborhood. She ran in a big loop through neighborhoods and liked to get most of her miles in, then stop and get her caffeine here on the way back and enjoy her drink as she strolled the last half mile and cooled down.

Once they reached the line of trucks selling various food and refreshments, she finally took her earbuds out as she stopped in front of a coffee truck. "Would you like something?" Her tone was as neutral as her expression. She might as well have been running alone for the way she'd completely ignored him.

He tightened his jaw. No, he didn't like this Isla at all—this Isla that he had created with his cold indifference. He was the one who'd put this wall between them, this distance. He shouldn't even be here with her right now, but after seeing her last night, he'd been powerless to stay away. It had been the first time he'd seen her in person since...everything. Telling the doctor he didn't want to see her had been hard, but once he'd left the hospital and thrown himself into work—and feeling sorry for himself—it had gotten slightly easier to keep his walls up. Seeing her in person, however? It had stripped him of all control, punched home exactly how lonely he was. He'd just been existing without her, his world dull and gray. It also made it clear how deeply he'd hurt her.

He pulled out a twenty from his shorts pocket and handed it to the woman behind the counter as he ordered for both of them.

"You didn't even ask what I wanted." Now her tone was no longer neutral, but tart as her pretty green eyes narrowed at him. Her auburn hair was pulled up into a ponytail, the braid hanging neatly down her back.

"Did I get your order wrong?" He knew his woman liked café Cubano. *No.* She wasn't his anymore. And he wasn't her anything.

She turned away from him as he got their drinks and paid, but she did take the small offering. And when her lips curved up in pleasure as she inhaled, he felt that smile all the way to his core. Damn, he'd missed her so much. Living without her was impossible.

But how could he saddle her with him the way he was now? He couldn't. But maybe...she could forgive him enough to be friends. At least then he wouldn't lose her completely. He could still be in her life, even if on the periphery. Which made him selfish, but there it was. "So how are things at work?" She'd taken on a lot when her father had— He couldn't even think it. He'd been friends with Douglas and it was his own fault that Isla's father was dead. His security was stellar but the bomber had found a hole, had exploited it. And innocent people had paid. It was all his fault, something she had to understand. And if she didn't now, one day it would set in. He knew that much.

He shook off the thoughts. Otherwise the darkness would creep in and consume him. At the moment he was with Isla, a bright shining star, and he wanted to bathe in her light for as long as she would let him stay with her.

"Good enough," she said quietly. "I'm hoping to wrap up the deals my father had in place before the end of the year."

There was a weird note in her voice, one he couldn't decipher. But he didn't like it and he wanted to put a smile on her face. To wipe away all the tension.

"I'm sorry I showed up on your doorstep like an asshole last night."

She made a snorting sound that was very un-Isla-like as she looked up at him. "You were kind of crazy last night."

Yeah, well, he'd never been sane when it came to her. From the moment they'd met, he'd fallen—hard. The last couple months without her had been hell. "I'm well aware."

"It's just about as crazy as renting a condo right across from me. What are you doing, Evan? Are you trying to hurt me more?" The exhaustion on her expression cut into him.

He rubbed a hand over his head. "No. The last thing I ever wanted to do was that—though I know I did. I did not handle things between us well."

"That's an understatement." She softly blew on her drink as they walked down the sidewalk, not looking at him anymore.

"If I could go back, I would do things differently. I would do a lot of things differently." He would have let her see him, then he would have ended things in a proper manner. Not...just cut her out. Not been such a coward.

"So...why rent the condo across from me?" She slowed down, careful with her drink as she stretched her arms and shoulders. "You showed up last night and ambushed me, then ambushed me again this morning. You refused to talk to me or see me months ago and now you're all up in my face? What's going on in your head right now?"

"I just...I'm kinda screwed up right now," he blurted out, but it was the truth. "I want to be friends again. I want to make up for what I did." The words were weak, pathetic, and he knew she would never let him back in after what he'd done. But just maybe, she'd give him her friendship.

The look she shot him was unreadable as they neared the front of her building.

It looked as if she wanted to respond but then she paused, frowning, and he looked over to see what she was focusing on.

Geno Conti.

That bastard. Evan felt his anger rise but ruthlessly shoved it back down. He had no reason to be angry but he wanted to know why the hell Geno was showing up at Isla's place on a Saturday. And wasn't that an ironic thought.

Refusing to leave yet, Evan nodded politely at Geno, managing to keep his civil mask in place as he watched the other man—who was looking between the two of them curiously. Conti had a little white bag in his hand

with the sticker of a local café on the front. He was bringing Isla food?

Hell. No.

*Breathe,* he reminded himself. *Also, don't punch him in
the face.*

"Geno. Surprised to see you again so soon," he said
mildly.

Geno paused, then took the hand Evan held out. Today Evan didn't squeeze it as if he wished it was the man's
throat. See? He could keep his impulses in check. Barely.

"I'll see you upstairs," he said to Isla, not caring what
Geno made of that as he stepped into the building.

He shouldn't be surprised that some rich, pretty-boy
asshole was sniffing around his woman... Except she
wasn't his.

*Damn it.* Maybe if he reminded himself of that
enough, he'd believe it.

\* \* \*

Isla stared at Geno in surprise, even as she found herself annoyed by the words Evan had tossed over his
shoulder. He might as well have peed in a circle around
her for how he was trying to stake a claim in front of
Geno. She wasn't sure what was going on with him and
his statement that he wanted to be friends again.

*Ugh, friends?* After what they'd shared? After being
engaged? After the way he'd hurt her? She wasn't sure
she was that evolved.

"Is everything okay?" she asked Geno, who was standing there, acting kind of nervous, which seemed out of the ordinary for the polished, charming man.

Wearing slacks and a button-down shirt, he looked as if he'd stepped off the cover of a glossy magazine. She wasn't sure how he always managed to appear so put together, but she'd never seen him with a hair out of place.

"I stopped by to bring you breakfast and see if maybe I really did have a chance with you. But I apologize, I didn't realize that you and Evan were..."

"We're not back together. At all. But..." Why did this have to be so awkward? She didn't like being put in this position but she generally liked Geno—this whole episode with him showing up at her place aside—so she was going to let this go. "I told you last night I wasn't interested and I feel like you're a fairly astute guy. So why are you here?"

He shoved out a breath and rubbed a hand over his perfectly thick, dark hair. "You're the first woman to treat me like, I don't know, not like the loser partier my family expects me to be."

Her eyes widened in surprise. "Well...you did a really good job of creating the partier persona for yourself." Over the last few years, he'd been splashed all over the tabloids, occasionally with actresses or other Miami socialites. Though to be fair, she didn't remember seeing much about him in the last few months. Maybe even longer.

"I know. Trust me, I know. My sister reminds me of that daily."

"So, what—you thought being with me would improve your image?"

He rubbed the back of his neck and shrugged, his cheeks reddening just the slightest bit. "Kinda, yes. I don't want to be that guy. The one known for being a lush, for being useless. Over the last year, since taking over this new division, I've done a lot of good, and it feels, well...good."

"If you don't want to be that guy, then don't be him. You don't need me to clean up your image. Just stop choosing the wrong women, stop getting in the news for the wrong things." And holy hell, she was done giving advice. This was not her deal and she was not his therapist.

"Those are wise words." He held up the bag for her, that affable smile sliding back into place, and she could easily see why so many women fell for him. But he did nothing for her. "I got this for you. Found out from your assistant what you like. You're not allergic to anything, are you?"

She lifted an eyebrow and took it in surprise. "That was very thoughtful. And just strawberries, so unless this has them, I'm good."

"Look, I hope things aren't awkward between us. I know if they are, it's completely my fault. Coming here was misguided and stupid."

Reaching out, she grasped his forearm briefly. "It's not either of those things." Okay, it had been stupid but she wasn't going to throw salt in his wound. "You live in some pretty big shadows," she said, referring to his father and older brother. Both of whom she'd interacted with on multiple occasions. They were nice enough but she could see why being the youngest would give Geno a complex. And yeah, it wasn't her role to soothe his ego, but whatever—he seemed sincere and she didn't have it in her to be a jerk to him. "You've done a lot in the last year, and it's impressive. I hope we get to work on more projects together. And I hope you won't be asking me out again."

"So blunt," he murmured, a ghost of a smile on his face. "I won't—and I hope we get to work together again as well."

They talked about their project, making awkward-ish small talk for thankfully only another minute before she was able to extricate herself.

This morning had been the weirdest morning she'd had in a long time. First Evan, and then Geno.

She wasn't sure what to make of Evan's declaration about friendship and forgiveness, and she wasn't going to obsess about it.

Much.

*Liar, liar,* she chided herself. That was all she was going to do for a while. Obsess over Evan because she simply couldn't get him out of her head, and seeing him had made things even harder. Especially since he'd been so apologetic, asking for her friendship. Even if he wasn't trying to mess with her head, he was still doing a pretty good job of it.

It didn't take long for Isla to shower and get changed before heading out again. Thankfully she didn't run into Evan on her way out.

Two Saturdays every month she tutored at a local community center where she taught reading. She'd been shy and awkward growing up and hadn't truly grown into her own skin until college. Books had saved her life as a kid. They'd been her escape, and she believed teaching kids to read was one of the best things you could do for them. Heck, for anyone.

Knowledge gave you power. And once you had knowledge, no one could take it away from you.

She hurried inside to be greeted by Marcy, the woman who ran the place.

Marcy's dark corkscrew curls bounced everywhere, her equally dark eyes flashing with warmth. "Isla, I'm so happy to see you. And you're early, of course."

She laughed lightly. "I can't help it. It's in my blood." According to her father, if you weren't fifteen minutes early, you were late.

"I've got two new students for you today. Both really sharp. One loves math and the other history—but they're struggling with reading and finding a subject that holds their interest. The first one will be here in twenty minutes and then I've got another one the hour directly after that. We're pretty full with tutors today, so as of now I've only got the two kids for you."

"Sounds good. I'm going to go put this in the break room." She'd brought a little snack bag with yogurt and cheese. Lately everything tasted like cardboard but she was forcing herself to eat.

She nearly jerked to a halt when she saw Evan in the break room, putting a reusable water bottle in the fridge.

"You're tutoring again?" she blurted even though yeah, it was pretty obvious.

"Yeah." His expression was neutral as he straightened. "I realized I needed to stop feeling sorry for myself. I didn't know you'd be here this morning—I'm not trying to cramp your style." And then he was gone, stepping out of the break room on silent feet despite his big size.

She blinked at his quick disappearance, feeling...lost. This community center was where they'd met. But after the bombing, after his injury, he'd stopped coming completely. According to his mother, he'd stopped going out anywhere for the most part. Preferring to hole up and work himself to death.

She was glad he was starting to get out more, even as anger and many buried emotions bubbled up. She'd tried to keep her walls up today, to shut him down, but it was hard. Being around him brought back far too many memories, and this morning she'd seen a peek of the Evan from before. The Evan who'd loved making her laugh—the one who'd stolen her heart and had made her feel safe.

Shaking off those thoughts, she put her bag in the fridge and headed toward the tutoring room. Right now she needed to get over her own issues and focus on what was important.

She couldn't even think about how she was going to handle Evan until later.

# CHAPTER SIX

"Isla, it's so good to see you," Rosa said as she stepped back, letting Isla inside her mother's home.

Her mother had a chef on staff but Isla had recently hired Rosa, a very qualified nurse, to live at her mother's estate. Her mom had no idea that Isla had vetted Rosa so thoroughly, and assumed the woman was simply over-seeing things in her deceased husband's absence. Though she was doing that too. "It's great to see you. How is she today?"

"Very well. She's only had a couple drinks."

Long ago Isla had given up the notion that her mother would stop drinking. Sophia McDonald didn't consider herself an alcoholic and Isla couldn't force her to quit. It didn't matter if she threw away every single bottle; her mom was a grown woman and would get more. Not to mention she was very good at hiding bottles. But it made Isla feel better to know that someone lived with her now and could keep an eye on her. And Rosa had run the entire maternity ward of an Orlando hospital for three decades. If anyone could take care of her mom, it was this wonderful woman. It was a strange thing to look out for one's own parent but it was what it was, and she was learning to accept it. She also realized she had a hell of a lot of privilege to even be able to hire someone to watch out for her mom.

"Good." She gently squeezed Rosa's outstretched hand. "I feel so much better knowing you're here."

Rosa nodded and paused, watching Isla for a long moment. "She's not alone today."

"Did one of her new bunco partners stop by?" Her mom had taken to bunco and found a whole group of girlfriends, very much unlike the socialite women she'd been forced to hang out with because of Isla's father. For the first time in ages, whenever Isla saw her mom, she was relaxed. Even with her father now gone, her mom hadn't spiraled into a drinking binge like Isla had feared—expected, even. This woman was...different from the mom she'd grown up with. She wasn't wound as tight, as anxious.

"Evan is here." Rosa's expression was very carefully neutral.

Isla plastered on a neutral smile of her own, even as her stomach curled into a hard ball. "Is he now?" What the hell was he doing showing up here?

"Your mother invited him and just told me before he arrived, or I'd have let you know sooner."

"Thank you for the heads-up." It might not give her much time to steel herself against seeing him, but it was better than nothing. She'd found herself running into Evan Bishop far too often the last two days. It had jolted her out of her routine, her misery, and pulled her out of her safe little bubble. More like sad little bubble where all she did was work and feel sorry for herself. *Pathetic.*

Minutes later she found her mother and Evan sitting on the lanai, her mom drinking a vodka martini and

Evan sipping a glass of ice water. He gave Isla a heated look that he quickly masked as he stood to greet her.

"Evan, Mom," she said, fake-ass smile firmly in place.

Evan surprised her by approaching and gently hugging her as he murmured in her ear. "She asked me and I couldn't say no."

The gentleness of his words and his embrace threatened to undo her, but she remained stiff in his hold. He was one of the few people who knew about her relationship and issues with her mother. Most people didn't even know about Sophia's drinking issue. Nope. Her image was carefully curated.

Of course he wouldn't say no to Sophia. Isla's mom, former beauty queen who'd snagged the eye of business magnate Douglas McDonald, was used to getting her own way. Isla was no different when it came to her mom—she found it hard to say no too.

"It's okay," she said quietly as she stepped back, desperate for space between them, her body aching from that simple embrace she'd been dying for these past couple months. Then she kissed her mom on both cheeks, forcing her feelings down deep inside. "You look stunning as always."

No matter what, she complimented her mom's looks. Her mom needed the ego boost more often than not, something Isla had a hard time understanding when she was one of the most beautiful women Isla knew. Inside and out. And on the outside? She still had killer curves, a beautiful smile and miles of long, thick, chestnut-colored hair. Isla had definitely not taken after her mother in the looks department. She was more willowy and slender, where her mom was all curvaceous vivacity and had a larger-than-life type of beauty reminiscent of long-gone Italian actresses. And outer beauty aside, her mom was on the board of two major charities—one of which helped abused women trying to start over and another that helped provide families in South Florida with fresh, healthy food.

Even with Evan here—or maybe because he was here—things felt weirdly normal. Like old times. She looked over the precisely set up spread of fruits, cheeses, and drinks already on the table. Her mother always alternated water and alcohol because she liked to stay hydrated. Always the beauty queen.

"It's so lovely to see you two together again," her mom said, smiling sweetly at them, but there was a glint of something in her dark eyes.

Isla hid a wince at her words. They weren't together, even though her mother simply meant in the physical proximity sense. But Evan smiled back politely and Isla picked up a little plate and started adding fruit to it.

"I'm happy to be here. It's been too long since I've seen you," Evan said. "And I owe you an apology for not coming by sooner. I'm so very sorry." He took her mom's hand and squeezed once and Isla knew he was being genuine.

She could see it in every line of his body. Evan and her father had been working on a deal to buy up a Southeastern transportation company with the hopes of expanding it nationwide, but they had also been friends, which just made Evan's ghosting act so much worse.

"Oh honey, you have nothing to be sorry for." Her mom patted Evan's hand gently. "You were going through your own dark time, something I understand."

"I don't deserve your forgiveness," he murmured.

She patted his hand again. "I received your condolences, so that's enough about that. How have you been getting along? Do the doctors say you need to worry about anything long-term? You look great, regardless," her mom added.

Sophia might have had moments of volatility throughout Isla's childhood, but deep down she was very kind. She'd grown up hard, had been raised by an alcoholic herself and suffered a lot of physical abuse. And she'd never felt like she fit in with all of her father's friends. Not when they all considered her an airheaded beauty queen. But she'd outlasted the first wives of all her father's business associates, something she was quite proud of. Her father might have been a hard man, but he'd loved his wife deeply and had indulged her every whim.

"Decently," Evan said. "I got lucky compared to a lot of people." His expression darkened then, and Isla imagined what he was thinking of.

"What about you, Isla? I hear through the grapevine you've been very busy. I also hear you might be dating Geno Conti," her mother said boldly. "That man is just the sweetest, certainly a charmer. I danced with him twice at a gala not long ago and he was so amusing."

Isla nearly choked on her cucumber water, surprised at the glint in her mom's eyes. Oh, she had set this up perfectly, Isla abruptly realized. Sometimes she didn't give her mom enough credit.

She smothered a laugh as she realized what her mom was doing. She was making it perfectly clear to Evan Bishop that Isla had moved on and that she had options. And she wasn't being very subtle about it. Isla shouldn't have expected anything less. Her mother might have issues, but she was ferocious when it came to Isla.

"I'm not dating anyone." She avoided looking at Evan. "Though when that changes, I'll be sure to let you know. Now tell me about this trip I hear you're planning."

"Rosa told you about that?"

"Of course. It sounds fun."

When her mom launched into her upcoming plans for a cruise with her bunco friends, Isla smiled. For the first time in two months, her mother was laughing and smiling and Isla was so grateful for the change. She knew her mother was an alcoholic and would likely never acknowledge that or change. But loving someone sometimes meant accepting them for who they were. If she had been toxic or dragging Isla down, it would be a different story. But her mom was who she was. And Isla was in a new phase of life where she was learning to let things go—namely the past.

Her mom was keeping her shit together better than Isla was, it seemed. Because right now Isla felt like she was drowning in grief over a man she could never be with again. Over a future that wasn't going to be hers.

\* \* \*

"She seems to be doing well, considering everything," Evan said as he walked Isla to her car an hour later. "And she's drinking less."

"She's really shown a tough spine through everything. And she's got this new group of friends that have been amazing. I wish she'd found them years ago."

He lifted an eyebrow.

"What?" she asked.

"Nothing, you just seem...more settled about her." It used to stress Isla coming over here. Today she'd seemed oddly settled, even with him there.

"I've finally accepted that I can't change her habits. She has to want to change herself, and if she never does, then so be it."

"Very true... She's one of the toughest women I know." His words must have surprised her because he saw the shock clearly on her face. "What?" he asked. "It's true. She survived the sharks of the Miami social scene for decades and everyone adores her. When she chairs something, people show up and donate. She's done a lot for the city." His own mother had commented on it more than once.

And while he might stay out of social bullshit as much as he could, he still had various businesses to run. He had his hands in transportation, tech, security, real estate—

including hotels—and even some small media production companies. He kept his ear to the ground about everything because he never knew when a kernel of information might be important.

"I wish she would see her own worth. Though I will say she was there for me after..." She cleared her throat. "She was there for me more than I was there for her after my dad died. She was a rock."

Though he knew she didn't mean to hurt him, it still hurt nonetheless. He should have been her rock. Instead, he'd simply contributed to her pain. "Isla—"

She leaned up against her car, arms crossed over her chest. "No. I can read you perfectly. No more apologies. I...don't want to hear them."

"Well I'm still sorry," he rasped out. He placed one hand on the top of her car as he looked down at her, dying to touch her. Kiss her. Hold her the way he wanted to. What he wouldn't give to be able to call her his again. "I should have been there for you."

She met his gaze now, tears shimmering brightly, and her pain hit him like a sledgehammer. "I should have been there for *you*. I *wanted* to."

"I know you did. And I'm sorry I shut you out." Instinctively he reached up and cupped her cheek. Because it felt natural, right. Because he'd done it hundreds of times.

For a moment suspended in time, she started to lean into it and then she froze, her eyes going wide. He froze too—what the hell was he thinking? Well, he was thinking that he wanted to lean down and brush his mouth

BISHOP'S QUEEN | 67

over hers, that he wanted to pull her tight against his body and never let go.

He abruptly dropped his hand and tried to figure out what to say. Before he could form any words, she turned away from him and opened her car door. Without another word she slid into the front seat and shut the door on him.

Torn, he stepped back and watched her car head down the driveway, and he couldn't help but feel like he was losing everything in that moment. He'd already lost her, but for some reason, today things seemed more final. Now that he'd finally talked to her, he was face to face with the reality of what he'd done.

What he'd lost.

Soft footsteps behind him pulled him out of the moment. When he turned, he found Sophia McDonald walking toward him, her kimono-style dress fluttering in the wind.

"I never took you for a coward," she said.

He could see himself in the reflection of her oversized sunglasses as she looked up at him. Petite and curvy, she was a force of nature.

He glanced away. "Yeah, neither did I," he muttered.

"If you think she's going to wait around forever for you to pull your head out of your ass, you are a fool." There was no malice in her words, just a matter-of-fact declaration.

"I know she's not going to wait for me."

"Are you sure about that? How are you going to feel when she moves on? Truly moves on. Because she will. That girl is a diamond. Someone will scoop her up."

He tightened his jaw and looked back at her. "She doesn't deserve to be saddled with me."

"At one time I thought you were the perfect man for her. And I'm definitely not talking about your looks. What you did was unforgivable. You broke her heart. It was so...*unexpected*. Of all men, I never imagined you would do something like that, Evan. I've never seen my girl so heartbroken. So I don't know how to answer you. I think if you want her, you need to go after her and be willing to accept her rejection. If you don't, you need to walk away. No 'let's be friends' nonsense. That would never work between the two of you. Both of you will only get hurt more than you already are." Surprising him, she patted him gently on the cheek. "I have faith that you're not completely stupid." Then she turned around and left him.

He wasn't so sure that she was right—because at that moment, he felt like the world's biggest dumbass.

He had to get his shit together, had to figure out exactly what his goal was. Because the truth was, he didn't think he could only ever just be her friend. He would always want more. Even if he didn't deserve it.

# CHAPTER SEVEN

A s she stepped into her condo, Isla smiled when she saw Jemma's name on her phone's caller ID. Jemma with her dark, wild, curly hair and infectious laugh, who'd been a rock for Isla the last couple months. They'd been close since college and the bond had never wavered.

She was busy feeling sorry for herself, however, so for a brief moment she thought about not answering, but she missed her best friend's voice. Heck, she simply missed her friend.

"Hey," she said, smiling before she even heard Jemma's voice.

"Hey yourself! What are you doing tonight?"

"Nothing, but—"

"Good. You're going out with me."

"Jemma, I don't feel like—"

"I don't care what you feel like. You need to get out, see real people. Interact with other humans. And I know you see people at work, but you have got to stop moping about Evan. And you need to be doing things that bring you joy—and that job isn't bringing you any freaking joy."

"I'm not moping." She felt more like she was grieving.

"I get it. I really do." Her tone softened just a bit.

Of all people, Jemma did. Her words weren't a hollow, useless sentiment. Jemma had been widowed at a

69

young age and had lost the love of her life. So...yeah, damn it, Isla hated it when her best friend was right.

"What do you have in mind for tonight?"

"A food festival not far from your place. I've got two tickets and I know a handful of people who are going to be there. So free food and drinks and you don't have to get all dressed up in a formal gown. Speaking of which, are you dating Geno Conti?" There was a note of horror in Jemma's voice.

Isla snickered. "No. He's not what the tabloids make him out to be though. He's really nice." The fact that Jemma was even asking reminded her that it had been a couple weeks since she and Jemma had done anything but text.

Her friend snorted. "Well, I'm glad you're not with him. So you're in tonight?"

"I'm in. We need to catch up anyway."

"Good, I'll pick you up at six."

"This better not be some weird date setup... Is it?"

"So distrusting." Then she laughed lightly. "Wear something sexy tonight." Jemma disconnected.

Isla frowned, setting her phone down. Jemma hadn't actually denied this was a setup. Isla was tempted to call her back but decided not to. She trusted Jemma. And the truth was, she did need to get out. She was either holed up in her condo or in her office at work, and she only attended work events—or visited her mother. She hadn't died; she and Evan had simply stopped being a couple.

She needed to accept it. And she needed to prove to herself that she believed it. It was the only way she was truly going to move on.

\* \* \*

"Thank you for tonight," Isla said as Jemma pulled up to the front of her building. She'd eaten tons of great food and laughed for a couple hours straight. She felt alive again for the first time in months.

"I had fun. And I've missed you," Jemma said pointedly.

"I know." She leaned her head back against the headrest. "I just thought... I don't know, I thought you were going to try to push me to date."

"Hell no. You don't need a man to be satisfied—there are toys for that," she added, laughing.

Isla grinned. "I feel like I've been living in a fog the past couple months."

"I get it. And even though it's not the same thing I went through, you are definitely in a state of grieving. I swear I'll never push you to date. That's your own business. I just...miss my friend."

"I've missed you too... Evan showed up at my mom's for brunch earlier today," Isla blurted out.

Jemma's eyes widened as she shifted in her seat. Her long, flowy cream and navy blue maxi dress rustled against the leather seat. "What? How is this the first I'm hearing about this?"

"I wanted to have fun tonight and not talk about him or think about him at all." She'd just wanted girl time free of any sort of drama—and they'd had such a good time. Her stomach ached from all the laughing.

"Details, now." She glanced in the rearview mirror. "And no one is behind me, we're fine."

Isla glanced over at the front doors of her building. It was quiet tonight, with no one coming in or out, so she turned back to her friend. "Well, it's not actually the first time I've spoken to him recently. He was at a business gala I was at with Conti." Quickly, she ran over everything that had happened over the past couple days. When she was done, Jemma sat there wide-eyed.

"Sounds like Evan wants to be back in your life. Whether as friends or more, who knows." Jemma's lips pursed into an annoyed line.

"What should I do?" she asked, though she knew no one could really answer for her.

"I have no idea. Look, I always liked Evan. A lot. He treated you right and he was just a great guy. I always thought he was like this magical unicorn and I still can't believe what he did. And I wasn't the one engaged to him, so I can only imagine how much he hurt you. I don't think there's a right or wrong answer for this situation. Just...go with your instinct."

"You realize that's absolutely no help at all."

"Sorry." She lifted her palms up. "I really don't know what to tell you. For what it's worth, I don't think you should open your heart up to him right away."

"Yeah, I wasn't planning on it." Not ever again.

"Good. Now go get some sleep," Jemma said, leaning over to give her a tight hug. "It's late and I want to be home before midnight. Apparently I'm getting all old because I'm exhausted and dreaming of my pajamas."

Laughing lightly, Isla hugged her and got out. As she made her way through the glass doors of the brightly lit high-rise, she nearly did a double take to see Evan entering via side glass doors, looking down at his phone. In jeans, a T-shirt and light jacket, he looked...relaxed and casual. Nothing like the tense man she'd seen the last few days. This looked like the man she'd called her own—the one who'd warmed her bed every night, made her breakfast most mornings. The one who'd let down his guard around her.

For a second, she had the urge to duck right back out the front doors and hide from him because there was nowhere else to go in the giant lobby except toward the elevators. But he must've heard her footsteps because he glanced over and looked just as surprised as she felt when their gazes collided.

"Hey," she said, heading for the elevators. She waved at the nighttime security guy as Evan fell in step with her.

"You look great," he said, doing a quick once-over sweep of her, his eyes all smoldering heat.

Feeling her body flare to life at the unexpected, raw hunger in his gaze, she looked away. She was wearing a dress Jemma had actually given her as a gift. Not Isla's style, but it was a fun, flowy bohemian thing with spaghetti straps and bright pops of color all over it. While wearing it she felt not exactly like herself, but free and fun, something she'd been lacking the last couple months. Jemma always brought out the fun in her anyway. Lately all of Isla's responsibilities had been pressing in on her and tonight had eased something inside her.

Made her feel human again.

She cleared her throat, realizing she hadn't responded. "Thanks. I went to a food festival tonight. Where were you out so late?" she asked before she could think to rein in the question. She inwardly winced. It wasn't her business anymore and she couldn't believe she'd even asked him. "I mean—"

"I was at Evie and Dylan's. They invited me over for dinner and I ended up staying longer than I planned when my parents showed up."

She hated that she actually felt a sense of relief surge through her at his words. Why? Because she was irrationally pleased that he hadn't been out on some date. She shouldn't care at all, but that was the problem. She still cared far too much.

Ugh, why couldn't she just get over him?

"How was the festival?" he asked, looking back at the elevator doors.

"Pretty awesome. The food was incredible..." She frowned when she heard her cell phone ringing. She'd turned the volume down during the festival but it was so quiet as they waited for the elevator that it was impossible to miss. "Hold on," she murmured, glancing at the caller ID. When she saw that it was Logan, head of security at her office, she answered immediately. "This is Isla."

"This is Logan. There's been an issue down at the building. Someone set off the alarm to your office."

"A break-in?"

"I don't see anything taken and we haven't been able to get anything from the cameras. But we've shut down the building exits completely and I've called the police. The alarm was triggered in your particular office, so I wanted to call you personally. I'm sorry it's so late—"

"No, you did the right thing by calling me. I'm headed down there right now." She turned for the doors.

"I would tell you that's not necessary, but I know you're going to come anyway." His tone was dry.

He was right. "I'll see you soon."

"What's wrong?" Evan asked as the elevator doors swished open behind her.

"It seems there was potentially a break-in at my office. They've shut the building down." Not that it would matter too much. Only a handful of people would be working tonight and only because they'd had international video conference calls.

"I'm going with you."

"Evan—"

"Please don't argue with me. I don't like that you were mugged, and now this."

"Well the two things certainly aren't connected. We live in a big city. Stuff happens."

Shrugging, he pulled out his keys as they headed toward the door for the parking garage. Since she didn't have her car keys, she didn't argue with him about driving.

"So how's your sister enjoying married life?" she asked to make conversation once they were in his SUV—and needing to fill the silence.

"It definitely agrees with her," he said as they drove out of the parking garage.

She settled back against the soft leather seats as he pulled out onto the side street. Some weird part of her was glad that Evan was with her tonight even if things between them weren't normal. "Any news about Ellis?" she asked softly. His brother was missing and wanted for murder. Isla didn't think he'd done it, but the Feds sure did. She couldn't believe Ellis had actually just disappeared, but he had worked for the DEA, so if anyone could manage it, she guessed it was him.

"No, unfortunately." His jaw tightened and he didn't say more so she let the subject drop.

Turning away from him, she glanced out the window, watching the city fly by in a blur as he maneuvered his way through downtown. Being in this enclosed space with him was messing with her senses, especially since he was stepping up to help out. Just as he would have back when they'd been a couple. Him being here with her was too familiar. *Too much.*

She just hoped that whatever had happened at the office tonight was a misunderstanding, that someone had simply triggered the alarm by accident. With the two contracts she was trying to wrap up, she didn't want to deal with anything else on top of it.

# CHAPTER EIGHT

E van glanced across the lobby of Isla's building where she was talking to Logan Masters, the head of security. Then he looked back at Detective Duarte who he'd been talking to. "I don't like any of this."

He could tell the detective was thin on patience, but Evan didn't care. "We simply don't have the manpower to do a sweep of every single office in this building. It would be a complete waste of our already stretched resources. Especially when security isn't even convinced there was a break-in. Nothing is missing and no one is injured, and they are diligently monitoring the many security feeds," he said, his tone far too patient. Maybe even patronizing, but that was probably Evan just being angry. "It looks like a glitch. Ms. McDonald says nothing was missing from her office, and over the last month there have been random triggers of the security system."

Yeah, he knew all of that. He still didn't like it. "Is there any news on her mugging?"

The detective shook his head again. "No. And I don't expect there to be."

Evan knew all that too and it only frustrated him further but he simply nodded. "Thank you for your help." There was no reason to be a dick to the detective when he was just doing his job—and everything he said was completely true.

Since Isla was still busy, he strode across the lobby and pulled out his cell phone, but kept an eye on her. With how keyed up he was, he didn't like the thought of her being out of his sight. As soon as he hit call, he realized the time and winced. It would probably go to voicemail anyway.

To his surprise, Special Agent Georgina Lewis answered on the second ring, sounding fully awake. "Lewis here."

"Agent Lewis, this is Evan Bishop. I just realized how late it was."

"It's okay. I've had my office calls forwarded to my cell. I'm working weird hours right now. What's up?"

He'd spoken at length to the agent about the bombing at his building since she'd been the agent in charge of the investigation. Her credentials were solid and she had a long record of closing cases—and she hadn't brushed him off after the bombing when he'd reached out with questions. "There was a break-in down at Isla McDonald's office tonight."

"Is anyone hurt?"

He gritted his teeth. "Nothing was taken and only one alarm was set off."

She was silent for a moment. "I know she's got great security down there. Is there anything on any of the recordings?"

"Not that security can tell. They just called her as a courtesy to let her know what had happened and to come check out things. But she was mugged a few nights ago and...I guess I just don't like the feel of it." Even as he said the words aloud, he realized it was a stretch to connect the two incidents, especially when they were both seemingly random. He inwardly cursed himself. He shouldn't be calling an FBI agent over this.

"Have either you or she or anyone related to your two companies received any threats lately?" she asked.

"No. I mean nothing serious, anyway." Evan had his hands in a lot of businesses and his companies got random threats all the time, usually from pissed-off people who'd lost their job because of their own incompetence. But him personally? He couldn't think of anything.

"I'll look into this but it doesn't sound like anything you should be worried about."

He rubbed a hand over his face. "Thank you for taking my call."

"No problem. Look, you went through a big ordeal. A huge one, and you survived it. It makes sense that you're going to be worried about Isla right now. But I can guarantee you that the man who bombed your office is behind bars and he has had absolutely no communication with anyone. We've got John Nix locked down tight and I'm personally keeping tabs on him. He confessed to the crime and we have all the evidence to back it up. So you can sleep easier at night."

Well, he didn't sleep easier at night because he was alone and usually woke up sweating, remembering the blast that had changed his life and destroyed others'. Nix had been pissed at the world, very anti-establishment and anti-capitalist, and Evan and Douglas had gotten caught in the man's crosshairs. Nix had been angry about the transportation deal even though it would have created thousands of jobs nationwide and utilized electric vehicles. According to his "manifesto," Evan and all the others were part of the capitalist monster machine.

He thanked her again and then they disconnected. But he still felt unsettled, as if something was looming on the horizon that he couldn't see but could feel in his bones.

More likely than not it was simply guilt. Guilt that someone had gotten a bomb through his own security that had killed Isla's dad and many others.

He shut his eyes at the thought, willing himself not to think about it. He still couldn't believe Douglas was gone.

"Evan?" Isla's soft voice nearly made him jump.

Damn, he hadn't even heard her approach and that wasn't like him. Schooling his expression, he turned to find Isla standing there in a multicolored dress he'd never seen until tonight, a sheer wrap pulled tightly around her shoulders. That was when he realized how cold she must be. He slid off his jacket, and without asking wrapped it around her shoulders.

She seemed startled, but gave him a small smile. "Thank you."

He simply nodded, hating that she was actually surprised by the gesture. Though given his recent behavior, it wasn't exactly surprising. No matter how much he tried to tell himself that he could be her friend, he wondered if he'd always view her as his to protect. "Anything new?"

She shook her head. "No, and it doesn't look like anything was taken. My computer definitely wasn't breached. I'm going to have IT run another scan in the morning, but...I have a feeling this is just another glitch. Something's been going on with our security system."

He didn't like the sound of that at all. "I want to review your security feeds tomorrow—"

"Evan, my people have this under control. Logan is going to have Ollie review every single feed from tonight to see if the team missed something. And they're doing full scans of people who leave the building starting today through the end of the week. You know how good Ollie is. It's okay."

Yeah, he knew how good Oliver Mulaney was with anything tech related. Evan still didn't have to like the situation. But he nodded because this wasn't his business and she was doing everything the right way. He knew this had never been her dream, to take over for her dad, but she'd slipped right into Douglas's shoes and was excelling. None of that surprised him. "You ready to go, then?"

She nodded, looking exhausted.

Evan would give up his left arm to call her his again, but he shoved that thought down tight. He had no room for fantasy in his life right now. Instead of wrapping his arm around her shoulders and pulling her close to him, he simply headed out of the building with her. At least he could ensure she was safe tonight.

Being in his vehicle with her, surrounded by her sweet, familiar scent, was a mix of pleasure and pain. He didn't want to be away from her, even as he knew he couldn't be with her. Thankfully she didn't attempt to make small talk.

But as they reached her building, she suddenly blurted, "Have you been dating anyone?"

He nearly jerked the steering wheel. "What?"

"I know I don't have a right to ask. But I want to know."

"*No.* Isla... After you, no one could ever compare." And that was the truth. She'd completed him in a way he'd never imagined possible. Never even thought he would want. He'd always been a "take it or leave it" kind of guy when it came to sex and dating. In the Marines, there'd been no time for sex. Or not much anyway, considering he'd been deployed in the Middle East for most of it. He'd been too busy trying to stay alive in different war zones. Then when he'd joined his father's business, he'd been so busy trying to take over the world, as Isla liked to say. Neither of his siblings had gone into the family business, so he'd jumped straight into everything with his dad.

She was silent, looking out the window as he pulled into the parking garage.

And he didn't like that silence—it grated on his nerves, raking over his skin in sharp jabs. He felt like a toddler, wanting to demand all her attention.

There had never been true silence between them. Not the uncomfortable kind, anyway. Everything between them had been easy, as if they'd just been waiting for each other. They had arguments, sure, but they'd all been over benign shit.

The silence now was different, uncomfortable. This divide between them was too great, and though he knew it was his fault, he also knew he couldn't conquer the distance. And he didn't deserve to.

As he parked, he thought about asking her if she'd been on a date earlier but he held back. He didn't want to know the answer. He just wanted her safe—and in his arms, in his bed, in his life.

As they neared their condo doors, Isla finally turned to him. "Thank you for coming with me tonight. I appreciate it." Her words were stiff, overly polite.

He hated it. "Of course. Hopefully it's nothing," he said, though he couldn't get rid of the tingling at the base of his spine. At least he was right across the hall from her now. If anything happened, he'd be there.

"So how long are you planning on staying across the hall from me? It's kind of weird." She watched him expectantly, her green eyes clear.

"I don't like that you were mugged," he said bluntly, though that wasn't an answer at all.

"So you think moving in across from me will somehow keep me safe from…the world?"

He shrugged.

And she gave him an exasperated look. "I was able to care for myself for the last two months and all the years before you. So whatever misguided reason you have for moving in here, you can move right out." She set her jaw tight, the familiar stubborn Isla at the forefront.

"I like being close to you."

"Is that right? *You* like being close to *me*?" She let out an angry-sounding laugh. "Oh, that's rich. Because—"

"That's right!" He leaned down, not sure what the hell he was going to do to cut her off. Kiss her? God, what was he thinking? He started to pull back, then she grabbed him by the front of his shirt and yanked him down to her.

Her green eyes flashed in anger—and hunger—as her lips collided with his. What was she doing? What was he doing? He should pull away, but he couldn't. Instead, he threaded his fingers through her thick auburn hair, cupping the back of her head as she plastered herself to him.

He loved the sweet taste of her, had missed her for far too long. Every morning he woke up, expecting to roll over and see her, but his bed was always empty. And cold. He'd ached for her in that hospital room, even as he was the one who'd kept her out. And he'd continued to ache for her once he'd been discharged. He simply couldn't stop wanting her.

Needing her.

Without breaking the kiss, he reached behind himself and held his hand to the scanner. A second later, the door opened with a soft snick and then they were inside his place.

Though it wasn't really his place, but a sparsely furnished rental with the basics and a killer view.

He wasn't sure what they were doing, not really. He wanted to be friends with her, wanted her in his life, but he didn't want to saddle her with him. And he really didn't want her to have any regrets. "We should stop," he rasped out, surprised he was able to talk at all as he pulled back, his breaths coming in hard and shallow.

She slid off his jacket and tossed it to the ground. "Should we?" Her tone was tart as she stared up at him almost defiantly.

*Dammit.* He couldn't remember why they should stop as he looked into her bright eyes. He wanted her so much, had never stopped wanting her, loving her.

She reached for him again, this time for the bottom of his shirt, but he grasped her wrists, suddenly cold all over. He didn't want her to see more, to see the swath of ugly scars forever embedded into his skin. Eventually they would fade, and maybe he'd even get used to them. But that wouldn't be today.

She struggled against his hold for a moment, but then let go as he crushed his mouth to hers.

She met his kisses with the same intensity as him, hot and hungry. When she shifted her body and wrapped her legs around him, he pinned her against the wall. Groaning, he cupped her breasts through the sheer fabric of her dress, kissing her as if he was dying, as if he might not see tomorrow. As if this was the last time he'd ever get to touch her.

And it might well be.

When she reached between their bodies again and grasped at his belt, he took over. Feeling like a randy teenager, he shoved at his pants and boxer briefs before pushing her dress up to her waist.

He felt absolutely possessed as he cupped her mound. He could feel how soaked she was even through the flimsy material of her panties. It turned him on even more that she was already wet for him, just as hungry as he was.

She rolled her hips against his hand, her entire body trembling as he teased her clit through the material.

God, he wanted to imprint himself on her. He wished they were naked, completely skin to skin, but he couldn't be that vulnerable with her. Not now. Not ever. Never again. She'd had the whole Evan before. He wasn't going to give her this version of him.

She let out a strangled moan and bit down on his bottom lip as he slid the material to the side and eased a finger inside her. Another groan tore from his throat. She was completely soaked.

He caught her groan with a hungry kiss, and when she grasped his hard length in her long, delicate fingers he nearly lost it. It had been so long since he'd even touched himself. As if that part of him had died the last couple months. Now it was suddenly back to life with a vengeance.

"In me, now," she demanded, her voice unsteady.

In the back of his mind a little warning bell went off, telling him this was a mistake, but he ignored it as he slid another finger inside her. Normally they spent a hell of a lot more time with foreplay—and they were usually both naked—but she was ready for him. And he knew that she had an IUD so he didn't worry about a condom.

"Isla—"

"Now." The word was a needy, desperate groan as her inner walls tightened around his fingers.

He couldn't hold back any longer, couldn't stop this. Feeling possessed, he shifted so that his cock was positioned right at her entrance. But when he thrust inside her, he froze.

She was so damn tight, so perfect. And right now it was like coming home. He'd missed her so much. Burying his face against her neck as she wrapped her arms and legs tight around him, he shuddered, savoring this moment.

Memorizing it.

The first time they'd been together, they'd been similarly frenzied, and hadn't even made it to his bedroom, instead jumping each other on his couch.

This was different, but it reminded him of that first time he'd completely lost himself to her. He was afraid to move, afraid to ruin this moment. And he didn't want to embarrass himself.

It had been too damn long and the tight heat of her was almost too much.

She dug her fingers into his back, and even with his shirt in the way, he felt the dig of her nails. Silently she rolled her hips, urging him on.

The feel of her wrapped around his cock was everything, but he needed her to come first. He'd screwed up so badly where she was concerned and he felt desperate to make her climax, to give her the pleasure she deserved.

He reached between their bodies and began teasing her clit, knowing exactly what she liked.

She jerked against his touch, sucking in a sharp breath as he rubbed his thumb in gentle little circles.

He felt her inner walls contracting around him, faster and faster. His balls pulled up tight as he focused on getting her off. Making her happy, bringing her pleasure—they used to be his favorite pastimes. And he might be screwed up, but he wasn't completely broken. He knew how to get her off.

"Evan." The way she said his name, a cross between a plea and a prayer, nearly set him off.

He knew she was about to come right before she let go. Only then did he begin thrusting, knowing it would extend her orgasm even longer.

She clutched onto his shoulders, her groans of pleasure the most erotic thing he'd ever heard as he buried himself inside her over and over.

As she climaxed, he let go of the bare thread of his own control and emptied himself inside her, coming in long, hard thrusts. His own orgasm seemed to go on forever, all his muscles trembling by the time she loosened her slender legs around his waist and he came down from his high.

"Isla," he murmured, leaning down to kiss her as he pulled out of her—but she stepped away from him, adjusting her dress and avoiding his gaze.

It was like a cold draft rolled through the room as she turned away, giving him her back. He didn't know what to say as he zipped his pants up, didn't know how to stop her from leaving when she reached for the door.

"Please stay," he managed to get out. Okay, maybe he could find the words. "Just...don't go."

But she didn't respond. Instead she opened the door and stepped out to the hallway.

Leaving him.

It felt like she'd just reached into his chest and ripped his shattered heart out.

# CHAPTER NINE

He stared out over the glittering Miami lights, pushing down his rage. His fist clenched around the stress ball, once, twice, over and over.

Breathe, he ordered himself.

Isla could still be his. She *would* be.

He'd gone through so much to get her. Killed her father, nearly killed that smug bastard Evan Bishop. All the others had just been collateral damage—and the stupid Feds thought it was over business. Everyone did. He'd have gone after Evan again but that fool had ended things with her.

It was...unimaginable. But he'd left the man alone because of it. Not to mention going after Bishop might have made the Feds look even closer at the bombing. They had the actual bomber, had that case tied up neatly, but they had no clue he'd hired the guy. It still shocked him that Bishop had walked away from Isla after surviving.

She was perfect, everything he'd ever wanted. Even if she'd shot him down.

Evan should have just stayed away from Isla forever, but now...he needed to die. Once Bishop was truly gone he could make his move, make Isla his. There would be nothing standing in their way anymore.

Rolling his shoulders, he turned away from the window and strode to his desk. He had work to do. The bomber he'd hired to take out Evan Bishop wasn't talking, but he was going to make sure the man never did. With the information he had on John Nix, the bomber would never talk. Not if Nix wanted to keep his daughter safe.

He pulled up a picture of the little girl on his screen, one he'd taken from outside her school, and printed it out. After slipping on gloves, he picked up the picture and slid it into a plain white envelope.

He didn't need to put a message on it. Didn't need to do anything at all other than send it—just like he sent a reminder picture every two weeks. All recently taken pictures of the little girl.

As he leaned back in his chair, he thought about how Isla had looked earlier in the week, especially at the gala. Her hair had been pulled up, showing off her long, elegant neck. She hadn't been wearing much jewelry because she didn't need it.

She was the jewel. He wanted to wrap his fingers around her long hair, crush his mouth over hers, fuck her any way he wanted. And she would beg for it. Beg for his cock.

He'd even set up that mugging, hoping she'd turn to him for comfort.

But nothing. Not even a whisper of what had happened to anyone. It was all Evan's fault. If he was gone for good, she would be able to get over him. To move on.

Only...he didn't understand what she saw in Evan Bishop. Especially now. The man looked like a monster.

She could have anyone she wanted, but according to what he'd been hearing, she and Bishop were talking again.

He clenched his stress ball again, his fingers digging into the soft squish of it. And it did nothing to push back the voice inside telling him to take what he wanted.

What he deserved. He'd waited patiently for Isla. It was his turn.

He'd been keeping tabs on her, but it was time to make his move.

Time to take his due—her.

# CHAPTER TEN

With her bag of Thai food in hand, Isla smiled at her assistant as she passed by Carol's desk, walking into her own office. She'd been so busy at work today she probably shouldn't have even left for lunch but she had to start taking care of herself.

She could practically hear Evan's voice in her head telling her she'd lost weight—but she squashed the thought of him. After last night, after they'd hooked up against the wall of his condo, she felt hollowed out. Empty.

She wasn't embarrassed, but she felt regret for her lack of control. Or maybe not regret but...she sure didn't feel good about last night.

She wasn't sure what she'd been thinking. But when he gotten all in her face, she'd just needed to kiss him to shut him up.

And then when she'd gotten a taste of him, that oh so familiar taste, something inside her had sparked wild and out of control. The man was like a drug—addictive and sending her senses into overdrive. She'd needed to have him. Feeling him pumping deep inside her had been incredible. But now reality and exhaustion had set in. They were right back where they'd started.

Exactly nowhere.

98 | KATIE REUS

So she'd made the decision to keep him at arm's length. She'd deal with Evan for business stuff, but that would be it. Nothing more.

*Liar, liar.* Ugh. Why did her inner voice have to be such an annoying know-it-all? She wanted to tell Jemma about last night but her friend had texted her this morning telling her she had to go out of town on an emergency trip. So she was going to save everything for when they could talk in person.

As Isla set her bag of food down, she smiled to see a cookie on her desk, wrapped in plastic. There was a cute little note that said *eat me*, along with a smiley face.

She recognized the wrapping from one of the local vendors. And it was her favorite—peanut butter and chocolate chip.

Eat dessert first, Jemma always said. Maybe she'd somehow dropped it off? As Isla unlocked her desk drawer and pulled her laptop out, she heard a familiar voice from outside. And she also heard Carol telling Ollie that she was busy.

"I'm free," she called out, not bothering with the intercom. She really should sit and eat but she wanted an update on the security system ASAP. These glitches were getting frustrating.

"Hey, boss." Oliver frowned when he stepped inside, seeing her takeout bag and the cookie. "Ah, I can come back later. I didn't realize you were having lunch."

"It's fine." She started unwrapping the plastic. "Seriously, don't worry. And please don't call me boss," she said, laughing. "I'm assuming you have an update."

"Maybe—I think so. I've done a full scan of the security system and I think it's more than a glitch that's been setting off the alarm. From what I've found—" He half turned, frowning at the sound of a very familiar voice from the other office.

*What the hell?* Isla resisted the urge to groan at the sound of Evan's voice. Mainly because she needed to keep a neutral mask in place, especially in front of one of her employees. But really...stupid butterflies launched inside her, mixing with her annoyance. So much for keeping him at a distance.

"I don't care if she's not seeing people." Evan's heated voice carried through from her assistant's desk. "I need to see her."

Picking up the cookie, she bit into it. Chocolate and peanut butter were definitely going to be her therapy right about now. Because clearly Evan was determined to make her crazy. The flavors exploding on her tongue were pure heaven. She'd take the small things right now.

"Just give me a couple minutes," she said to Ollie, pushing up from her desk and setting the cookie down. She needed to deal with Evan quickly, then get back to business.

Taking a step around her desk, she stumbled as her throat closed up tight.

*Oh, God.* She knew what this was. Gasping for breath, she clutched at her throat even as she fell forward against her desk. Fear clawed at her as she tried to draw a breath and failed. *No, no, no.*

The cookie must have had strawberries—or traces of it. Which made no sense. But that didn't matter. Only breathing did.

She needed her EpiPen!

"Isla..." Ollie stepped forward, his eyes wide as he stared at her in horror. "What's wrong?"

"Isla!" Evan shouted, a giant blur of motion as he rushed into her office.

In one sweep he took in her face and the food on the desk. She tried to drag in a breath, but could only wheeze in the tiniest fraction of air as her throat swelled.

*Ohgodohgodohgodohgod.*

She stumbled back, knocking papers off her desk. *Have to get my EpiPen.* There was one in her purse but the one in her desk drawer was closer. Before she'd even taken two steps, Evan strode around the desk and yanked open the left-hand side drawer. Because of course he knew where she kept it.

Her knees buckled as she tried to draw in an impossible breath. As she hit the ground, he slammed the needle into her thigh and injected her.

Gasping, she felt the effects moments later and sucked in a deep breath of blessed air, dragging in breath after breath as her heart raced out of control.

"Call an ambulance!" he shouted.

She was vaguely aware of Ollie on his cell as Evan lifted her into her office chair.

"Look at me," he demanded as she collapsed back. "Talk to me. Are you okay?"

"Yes," she rasped out, adrenaline pumping hard through her. She blinked as she watched him, only able to focus on his face. She had no idea why he was here and she didn't even care. Because she wasn't so sure she would have been able to get to her EpiPen in time.

"The ambulance is on the way," Ollie said as Carol simply stared at her with wide eyes.

"Where did you get this cookie?" Evan asked, completely ignoring the woman.

"It was on my desk," she said. "I thought it was a gift from Madeleine or maybe Jemma."

"Who left this?" Evan demanded, turning back to Carol.

The other woman just stared. "I don't know," she whispered. "I had to go to the bathroom and I left my desk unattended." Now tears started flowing down her cheeks.

Even Ollie looked shaken, his cheeks and even lips gone pale.

She tried to tell Carol that it was okay even as Evan let out a savage curse. But Isla couldn't find the words.

He strode over to one of her cabinets, pulled out an envelope and dropped the cookie inside.

She wanted to ask him what he was doing but she had a feeling she knew even as the weird sensation spread down her spine. There was no way this was intentional, was there? The cookie shouldn't have had any strawberries though. And from the way she'd reacted? It hadn't been mere traces of it.

Closing her eyes, she leaned back against her chair as Evan ordered her assistant and Ollie out of the room like a drill sergeant.

She might not want to go to the hospital but she knew she needed to in case she had a second reaction once the epinephrine wore off. Right now, she was glad that Evan was with her.

\* \* \*

Isla stepped out of a small hospital room, only momentarily surprised Evan had even been able to get something private, but she probably shouldn't have been. The Bishop name had a lot of pull in Miami.

"What are you doing?" Evan asked as he rounded the corner, clearly surprised to find her leaving the room.

"I'm going to get some of those little biscotti things I like." She hated it here—the smells, the memories of Evan shutting her out—but she'd gotten very familiar with the hospital layout when she'd been waiting for him to wake up from his coma. "Then I want to leave."

"There was strawberry in the cookie," he said, his expression growing darker.

"I kind of figured." It was the only thing she was allergic to. Unless she'd all of a sudden developed an allergy to chocolate or peanut butter—and she didn't think the universe would be so cruel right now. Luckily she hadn't had another reaction and enough time had passed that she was in the clear. "Can you start the release process? I don't want to stay here any longer." She knew she'd have to talk to the cops—again—but she was done with hospitals. So freaking done.

Frowning, he swept his gaze over her in a purely clinical fashion as if he thought she was going to fall down. He was being incredibly overprotective. And while she definitely appreciated it, there was nothing more anyone could do for her.

Reaching out, she placed a hand on the middle of his chest. "Look, I'm fine. I promise. Thanks to your quick thinking." A shudder snaked down her spine as she thought about what would have happened if Evan hadn't been able to get to her EpiPen in time. And as far as she knew, her assistant didn't even know where it was—something she was going to remedy soon.

"I don't like you just going off by yourself."

"I'm at the hospital surrounded by tons of people. Whoever poisoned me is a freaking coward." And she couldn't imagine who would have done it either. Security was looking into it, but so far she simply couldn't imagine someone trying to actually kill her. Because she would have died without her EpiPen.

"Fine. Just wait for me. I'll get the nurse and we'll grab the biscotti on the way out."

She was too tired to argue. She'd just wait until he was gone and do what she wanted. They weren't together anymore and some part of her needed to buck at his order. "Okay."

Surprising her, he leaned down and kissed the top of her head in a gentle action that rattled her so much she stepped back, needing distance from him. As soon as he was gone, she grabbed her bag and headed down to the first floor. He was being ridiculous, and she knew the ins and outs of this hospital—she'd stayed here long enough. Her shoes made little squeaks against the linoleum. She wasn't sure where Evan had snagged her sneakers from, but it was a relief to wear these instead of her heels.

As she passed by the bustling cafeteria, peeking inside and seeing it full, she continued down the hallway. There were a few vending machines with the biscotti she liked and she'd never been able to find them anywhere else. It had been one of the few things she could stomach when she'd been waiting for news on Evan. If anything, she almost felt a compulsion to grab some—they reminded her of the "Before." Before Evan had cut her out of his life and decided they weren't together anymore. Before her life had swerved onto a rocky path she never could have predicted.

Shoving away those thoughts, she stepped into the little alcove with a coffee bar and a machine with all sorts of food—most of it so-so. In the reflection a taller man wearing a hoodie stepped up behind her, crowding her personal space. She shifted to the side, annoyed at how rude he was being.

Suddenly a hand shoved into her back, propelling her forward against the machine. Stars danced in front of her eyes as the glass rattled under the force of her body.

She shoved off it, raising up her elbow to fight off this stranger, but he grabbed it in his meaty fist before wrapping his arm around her neck. A kaleidoscope of color flashed before her eyes as he tightened his grip, cutting off her air supply.

*No!* The voice in her head screamed as she tried to get the word out. He was squeezing too tight, too hard.

Flailing wildly, adrenaline and panic punched through her in equal shots. *No, no, no.* She refused to die here. Kicking out, she found purchase on the vending machine and shoved backward.

The guy grunted, his grip loosening, but not enough. She dragged in air, grateful for the oxygen, but before she could scream he went for her throat again. He wrapped one arm around it and shoved a hand over her mouth.

She shoved backward hard, taking him off guard. When he loosened his grip, she ducked out of his hold and ran, screaming as loud as she could as he stumbled behind her. Not looking back, she sprinted down the hallway, nearly running into two nurses who were stepping out of a swinging door marked *Employees Only.*

Her heart raced out of control as she jerked to a halt in front of them. "A man..." She dragged in air. "Choked me. Tried to kill me." She managed to get out enough words that one of them took off as the other pulled out a cell phone.

"Come with me," the woman said as she wrapped an arm around her, quickly ushering her down the hallway as she called security.

Isla needed to call Evan, needed— She swallowed hard as reality started to sink in. Someone had attacked her in the hospital. Someone seriously wanted her dead, and the concept was baffling and terrifying.

This wasn't random. It couldn't be. Just like the cookie couldn't have been random. Not after what had just happened. Now she really wished she'd listened to Evan when he'd told her to stay put.

# CHAPTER ELEVEN

"What are we doing here?" Isla asked as Evan pulled up to his building. He'd insisted on leaving the hospital almost immediately.

She was still ice cold, unable to get rid of the chill that had settled deep in her bones and wouldn't abate. Her throat was sore and she felt more exhausted than she could ever remember being. As if she'd just run a marathon. She thought about calling Jemma or her mom, but didn't want them to worry.

"We're staying at my place for now. It's more secure. The rental is fine but I like my security better than yours. And after what's happened, you need to be far away from home. From any routine." His fingers were gripped tightly against the wheel, his knuckles gone white under his hard grip.

His security actually was better and his place was bigger—and she agreed with everything he'd said. Still. "You didn't feel like asking me first?" Her tone was mild as she glanced over at him, unable to muster up any sort of annoyance right now. Not when she was still trying to deal with what had just happened.

His jaw tightened as he pulled into the parking garage, but he didn't actually respond.

"Oh my God, you didn't want to risk me saying no, right?" She couldn't even be surprised.

He lifted a shoulder in response.

She shoved out a breath of annoyance. "Look, I agree with you. Your place is more secure. But asking me would have been appreciated." She didn't like feeling bulldozed, having control taken away from her. Especially now.

"I want to apologize, but I'm not actually sorry." Pure protectiveness flashed across his expression.

She stared at him for a long moment and let out a startled burst of rusty laughter that felt foreign given the terror of what she'd just gone through. "At least you're being honest."

The tension in his shoulders eased only a fraction as he parked. "Detective Duarte might already be upstairs waiting. I told security to let him through if he got here before us."

They'd left the hospital almost immediately, with Evan insisting she would be safer away from there—and security hadn't been able to stop him. The man was a force of nature when he wanted something, and today she was grateful for that. She hadn't wanted to stick around the hospital while the police searched for the man who'd attacked her—the man who had no doubt escaped already.

She'd started to respond when her phone started ringing. Geno's name flashed on the caller ID and she almost ignored it as she stepped out of the passenger seat—then remembered she'd missed their meeting today. "Geno, I'm so sorry—"

"Don't be sorry. Carol told me what's going on. She said you had an allergic reaction...and then someone attacked you at the hospital?"

She closed her eyes for a moment as they reached the elevators. She wasn't surprised Carol had been so forthcoming, but wished she hadn't told him about the hospital attack. She'd let her assistant know what was going on so she could hold all her calls and deal with any potential issues. "Yes, it's true. And I'm about to talk to a detective. Can I call you back in half an hour and fill you in on everything?"

"Of course. I'm glad you're okay. Let me know if you need anything."

After they said their goodbyes and disconnected, she tucked her phone into her purse. She definitely needed to talk to Geno about some work things, and she was going to be pretty open with him about what was going on because he had a right to know since he would be spending time with her. But that was a conversation for later, when she was alone. Because if she was being honest, she did not want to have a conversation with Geno in front of Evan. Not when Evan had made it clear he didn't like the other man.

Right now she didn't have the energy to deal with anything extra.

Evan was right—Duarte was waiting for them by the time they reached the penthouse floor. He was silent as Evan unlocked his door and they all stepped inside, but his grim expression only added to the lead ball congealed in her stomach.

"Thank you for meeting us here," Isla said to him, mainly to break the silence as they moved into the living room. She sat, not trusting her wobbly legs to hold her up. Today's reality was starting to hit her. Hard. "Evan didn't really give me a choice." He shot an annoyed glance at Evan before focusing back on her, his expression softening.

"I wasn't keeping her at the hospital," he murmured, clearly not sorry as he sat next to Isla. If anything his expression was challenging, if not outright confrontational.

The detective continued. "We're taking all of this very seriously. The poisoning is very hands-off, but the attack at the hospital? That's... It's serious and violent, and I'm going to do everything I can to find who is behind it. I've already spoken to your head of security and we're going to be running through your security feeds. This feels very personal, nothing like what happened before." His gaze flicked over to Evan for a brief moment, the reference to the bombing clear.

She wrapped her arms around herself as she instinctively leaned closer to Evan. Isla might want to keep her distance from him, but she wasn't going to bother today. Not when he made her feel safe. "What exactly do you need from me?"

"A list of enemies. Any exes or bad dates you've gone on recently, anyone who has a personal grudge against you. And..." He looked at Evan again. "I'm going to need to talk to you as well. Any exes that might want to hurt Isla to get to you."

Evan shook his head. "I haven't dated anyone since Isla and I...broke up. And I wasn't serious with anyone before her. No one who would go to the kind of lengths this person has gone to."

The detective nodded once and wrote something on his notepad.

Her phone dinged again and she glanced at the screen. She'd received various texts from Carol, Ollie, Geno, and even Logan. Word had spread around the building about what had happened, so now it seemed everyone knew. And Logan had assured her they were completely revamping security after this and currently working with the police. But she didn't recognize this number. She pulled up the message and gasped.

"What?" Evan leaned over, and before she could respond he plucked the phone from her hands and held it out to the detective.

"You're going to pay, whore." Detective Duarte read the message out loud, his expression growing even darker.

Then he wrote something else down, the phone number from the screen, she guessed.

"Yes, this is personal. And I suggest you get some rest," he said, standing. "Whoever texted you probably isn't dumb enough to do it from their own phone but we're still going to run this number. We are going to find out who is behind all this. And I know I don't need to tell you this, but don't take any unnecessary risks. If you have a routine, mix it up. Don't go in public unless you have to. I know this is less than ideal, but until we've caught this guy, just be smart. And let your own security here know what's going on. No random deliveries allowed through, nothing."

Evan stood with him. "I'll be her shadow until this guy is caught."

There was a bite to Evan's tone that made the detective straighten. "Walk out with me?" Duarte asked.

And since he didn't include her, she didn't go with them. Instead she stood, stretching. She felt a thousand years old as she walked to the huge window overlooking downtown Miami. The sky was now fading into pinks and oranges as the sun descended. Today had gone by in a blur of insanity. She'd missed meetings, had emails and other crap to catch up on but...she didn't really care. At the end of the day, she was just glad to be alive. And she was really grateful to be with Evan, to be at his place and under his protection. She didn't care what it said about her either. She needed him right now, needed to not be strong and in control.

"I put in a call to Lizzy at Red Stone Security. She's got the security feeds from the hospital around the time of your attack," Evan said quietly from behind her a minute later. "She's sending them over to us to review."

Blinking in surprise, she turned to find him only a couple feet in front of her. "Did you tell the police?"

"No. I trust that they're going to do everything they can and they'll be reviewing the feeds too. But Lizzy didn't get them legally, and I'm not sitting on my hands. There's got to be enough video evidence from the hospital and surrounding buildings near yours downtown that she might be able to get something. Whoever sent that text is serious. They tried to kill you," he growled, stepping forward and pulling her into his arms.

She didn't fight his hold, wrapping her arms around him and burying her face against his chest.

She'd been trying to compartmentalize things the last couple hours, but she'd been poisoned and then someone had attacked her at the hospital. Her neck and body were still sore and she was having a hard time computing it all. Being in Evan's arms right now? Yeah, that helped ease some of her fear. He might have broken her heart, but he was here now and he was being a rock. This was the Evan she'd fallen for, the one who had been unflappable in the face of...everything. "I've called Rosa and told her to increase security at my mom's house. And Jemma's out of town and she's the only other person I can think of who someone would try to hurt to get to me."

"Good," he murmured against the top of her head. He didn't loosen his hold either, just held her tight.

And God, she'd missed him, missed his strong embrace. She closed her eyes for a long moment, inhaling his familiar scent. Even if she didn't want to depend on him right now, she was going to take what he was offering. She could admit that she was terrified. Not knowing who had come after her was even worse because she had some faceless enemy out there wanting to kill her.

"I wish I'd never gone for that stupid biscotti." Tears clogged her throat.

"This isn't your fault. And I'd never have left you alone for one second if I thought someone was lurking around the hospital waiting to... Waiting." He held her even closer, actually shaking as he gripped her tight. "We'll find the guy."

She certainly hoped so. But she knew things didn't always have a happy ending. And she couldn't stop the fear welling up inside her that told her all of this was going to end badly.

*  *  *

Restless, Isla stared at the ceiling before rolling on her side. She couldn't get comfortable, couldn't get warm enough. Then she was too hot. Even the luxury sheets seemed to chafe against her skin as she kicked them off. The place was fully insulated from the outside world, so she didn't even have the street noise far below as a distraction. Everything was so quiet—and that gave her too much time with her thoughts. She'd tried reading and television, but neither of those had worked to distract her.

She kept feeling that man choking her, trying to squeeze the life out of her. And being here, being in Evan's place—in his freaking *guest room*—was bizarre. Not as bizarre as what was going on in her life, but it was one more layer of weirdness on the shittiest cake ever.

It didn't matter that everything in the room was pure luxury for maximum comfort and had been designed professionally. The Swarovski chandelier above the California king-size bed was gorgeous even at night, but in the daylight it sparkled. Everything was done in soft grays, whites and silvers, giving the room an ethereal glow that reminded her of a spa. But it wasn't Evan's bedroom, and that was the problem.

Even after all he'd put her through, even after how badly he'd hurt her, she still wanted him. When she heard a soft chime, she glanced around the plush room until it registered that someone had texted her at…three in the morning?

Dread swelled inside her as she picked up her phone. *Oh no.* It was from a different unknown number.

*I'm going to enjoy slitting your throat, bitch.*

Bile rose inside her and she dropped the phone as if she'd been burned. Jolting out of bed, she didn't even think, she just headed straight for Evan's room. Pausing at the doorway, she swiveled back and plucked up the phone.

Her feet were silent against the long Persian runner that was warm underneath her bare soles as she moved. Barely a moment passed after she knocked before the door swung open.

"You okay?" Evan stood in front of her in a long-sleeved workout shirt and a pair of jogging shorts.

"Yeah, I…" She held out her phone, unable to fight off a shudder as the vile words replayed in her head.

He swore softly and stepped back. "Give me a sec." He grabbed his own phone and sent off a couple emails—to

Detective Duarte and Lizzy, she saw—before setting it back on his nightstand.

The room smelled like him, triggering a bittersweet pain in her chest. Once upon a time, she'd left her own phone, e-reader and other personal things on the opposite nightstand. Now that one was bare except for a lamp, everything gone as if it had never been. As if she'd never stayed here at all. Cold swept through her and she looked away, back at him.

"You're staying in here tonight," he ordered, leading her to what had once been her side of the bed.

"I..." She was going to say that she shouldn't, but right now she didn't care about what she should or shouldn't do. She didn't want to be alone, even if it muddied the waters between them even more. And that was when she realized he definitely hadn't been sleeping. His laptop was propped open, the soft glow of light bathing the pillow. "You're working?" She slid under the covers, careful not to jostle his laptop.

He shrugged and grabbed it off the bed, closing it. "Just looking over the security feeds." He dimmed the lights then slid in next to her.

His familiar, masculine scent teased her senses, but she ignored it. Or tried to. She felt safer just being next to him. She and Evan had their problems, but he would protect her no matter what, without expecting anything in return. "Find anything useful?"

She'd looked at some of them earlier but the attacker had been wearing a hoodie and then he'd just disappeared into one of the rooms. Detective Duarte had told them they'd done a thorough search of it and the entire hallway, but by the time they'd actually searched the room the man was gone. The assumption was he'd gone out the first-floor window since he hadn't been captured on any more cameras.

"No." So much frustration filled that one word. "I keep thinking if I watch enough, I'll see something, that his body language will look familiar. I don't know," he muttered, stretching out next to her.

Being in his bed again was just more weirdness, making her wish she could stay here forever. All safe and warm and tucked in where maniacs couldn't try to kill her. "The police will figure out who's behind this. Whoever is doing it isn't a ghost. They'll make a mistake." There was far more conviction in her words than her heart. If she believed it, maybe it would really happen—sooner than later.

"I'm sorry you're dealing with this." He reached across the divide between them and patted her hand gently.

She hated the distance and awkwardness between them. It felt wrong. "Thanks. Can I ask you something?" she blurted, knowing that her next words would likely cause tension and force her from the room. But she needed to know. "I know you said that you ended things because you didn't want me to stay with you out of pity—which for the record is stupid—but there's gotta be more, Evan. I want the truth." She turned her head, watching him lie there, his body tense, all his muscles pulled taut.

"I got your dad killed," he finally gritted out.

She blinked. "What?"

"If my security had been tighter, if that monster hadn't found a hole in it..." Sighing, he rubbed a hand over his face. "Douglas would still be here. Instead I'm all screwed up and your dad is dead. And it's my fault, Isla." He turned to look at her then, self-loathing and guilt glittering in his blue eyes.

"You're serious?" *That* was what he thought? A mixture of surprise and horror jolted through her. It wasn't his fault. "I don't blame you for that. I don't blame anyone but the man who killed him and all those others." And had hurt her sweet Evan.

His jaw tightened and he turned away, lying flat on his back again. "You say that now."

"I say that now and forever." She wasn't going to blame him for things outside his control, and to hell with him making stupid assumptions about her feelings.

He snorted, which just annoyed her. But she knew him well enough not to push. Not directly anyway.

She hadn't realized he'd been feeling such extreme guilt over her dad's death—and she could see it in his eyes tonight that he was. It was so raw and real and...

This changed everything.

She'd thought he'd simply pushed her away because he thought she couldn't handle his scars. And the shallowness of it had shocked her. This made more sense. And it also made her want to pull him into a hug and then shake some sense into him.

She'd thought she was done fighting for him, *for them.* Sighing, she closed her eyes. Maybe she'd never be done.

She still wanted this stubborn, maddening man. Apparently she needed to try a different tactic.

"Do you remember the day we met?" It had been at the community center, and he'd been so sweet and charming.

"Oh yeah. I sounded like a moron," he muttered.

She laughed. "No you didn't. You were adorable. I always wondered... Would you have ever called me if you hadn't run into me that night with my dad?"

He cleared his throat and the bedcovers rustled slightly as he shifted. "I actually set up that dinner."

"What?" She rolled on her side to look at him and thankfully he turned to watch her as well.

"Yeah. I called your dad, asked him to meet me for dinner and to bring you. I told him I was pretty sure I was going to marry you." He started to smile then, the hint of the easygoing, charming man she knew sliding into place before he abruptly turned away and stared at the ceiling once again.

"He never said anything," she whispered, beyond surprised that her dad hadn't ever told her. "Wait...you told him you thought you were going to marry me even then?"

He lifted a shoulder.

Okay, they were going to talk about *that* one day. "Why didn't you just ask for my number?" She was pretty sure she'd been putting out all the right vibes.

"Because you made me nervous."

"You were voted sexiest bachelor in Miami like...three times, I think." Maybe more.

"So? You intimidated the hell out of me, Isla."

She wasn't sure what to do with that, what to even say. So she backtracked. "I wish you'd told me you were living with all that guilt about the bombing." It would have saved them both a lot of heartache.

"I didn't handle things well. Do you think...we can ever work things out between us?"

"I don't know." Sighing, she closed her eyes, surprised at the exhaustion pressing in on her. Okay, not surprised, but she couldn't believe she was actually starting to doze, to let sleep pull her under.

She was with Evan, however. And no matter what, he made her feel safe in a way no one ever had.

"Get some rest," he murmured, his deep voice lulling her to sleep even more.

Tomorrow she could worry about...everything.

# CHAPTER TWELVE

H e told himself not to make the call.
*Don't call her. Do not do it.*

He shouldn't reach out but...he needed to. Needed to hear her sweet voice, that soothing cadence he craved. He'd been obsessed with her for too long, had finally gotten her to a position where they could be together. And then...nothing. But he wasn't giving up. He would never give her up. She belonged to him.

He closed the closet door and found his phone in the kitchen where he'd left it.

His fingers twitched over the screen. He shouldn't. He would. No...

He rolled his shoulders and pulled up Isla's name and face. He'd taken dozens of pictures of her that she had no clue about, but this picture was the standard one linked to her email. If she ever saw her profile on his phone randomly, he couldn't have her knowing about all his pretty, secret pictures.

She picked up on the third ring, sounding exhausted. "Hey," she murmured. "Everything okay?"

"Yeah, just checking on you. I know you had a bad day yesterday." He winced. Of course she'd had a "bad" day. An awful one. And whoever had tried to hurt her was going to pay with their life.

"I'm doing okay. I'll be in the office later, but I can pull up files if you need to discuss anything now?"

"No, I'm good." They had a meeting scheduled later that he wouldn't miss. "I was just making sure—" He stopped as he heard a familiar male voice in the background. Evan Bishop.

She was with him again? Of course she'd run back to him. Bishop had taken her to the hospital yesterday and hadn't even been able to protect her. But she must have stayed with him, or he with her, because it was barely seven in the morning. God, he couldn't even call her without this bastard interrupting them.

"Hey, I've got to go, but I'll see you soon?"

"Of course." He'd see her at the office later today since they had a meeting, but it wasn't enough. It was never enough. They would be so good together, if only she would open her eyes and really see him. He was so much more than she knew.

And lately he couldn't stand the limited time he got with her. He wanted more. As he hung up the phone, he stared out the window, not seeing anything in front of him as he digested that Bishop had stayed the night with her.

He just couldn't believe she'd gone back to him.

After the way Bishop had treated her, and now she was with him again. He'd seen the stupid article online but had brushed it away. But then Bishop had shown up at her condo the other day, then at work yesterday.

It was almost as if he'd shown up to save the day. But no, Bishop wouldn't have poisoned her.

He knew that for a fact—and he was going to find out who had done it. It wouldn't take long either. He simply had to pull up the real security feeds using a backdoor he'd installed to infiltrate the system.

Whoever had hurt her was a problem he was going to have to take care of. Personally. But he couldn't forget that Isla had returned to Bishop. He clenched his jaw, trying to shove down the rage inside him.

He'd given her so many chances to be with him—had asked her out, was trying to be a shoulder for her to lean on.

In the end she'd gone back to that asshole Bishop. Bishop, who should be dead.

He heard a cracking sound and when he looked down, realized he'd crushed the remote control for the ceiling-to-floor-length curtains, now open to reveal a view of downtown.

He tossed the pieces blindly to the floor and headed back to his bedroom. Rage simmered beneath the surface, no matter how hard he tried to keep it at bay. He felt as if she'd betrayed him. And after he'd maneuvered things so much, so they could finally be together.

In his room, he opened his closet again and looked at the picture of Isla tacked directly in the middle. He had so many of her, but this one was his favorite. It was from the recent gala she'd attended. She'd been laughing at something someone said. He wasn't sure who, and he didn't care, but seeing that laughter on her face after months of nothing but sadness—she had lit up the entire room again. He used to want to see her smile all the time, but... He shook his head once and scrubbed a hand over his face. She was screwing Bishop again. She had to be if he was staying with her.

*No, no, no.*

He slammed his fist into her picture, the plaster cracking behind it, the image crinkling with impact. He had to confirm it, but if she had truly gone back to Bishop...he wouldn't let this stand. No one said no to him.

And she was done betraying him. He was done letting her.

# CHAPTER THIRTEEN

E van frowned as he continued scanning through one of the many security feeds Logan had sent over. People were moving around like normal, there weren't any weird glitches in the— Oh, hell. That was it.

Isla had been wearing a different dress yesterday. This was definitely an old feed. So whoever had delivered that laced cookie had access to security. Or hacked into it. *Shiiiiit.* They'd been able to move around freely without anyone's eyes on them.

Isla had already told her people to give Evan whatever he wanted, so he grabbed his cell phone and called the security office.

"This is Ollie."

"Hey, it's Evan Bishop. Is Logan there?"

"No. I'm working on an audit on all of our feeds and something is wrong," he said. "Isla said we could loop you into anything. I found something and it's why I came by to see her yesterday. How's she doing, by the way?"

"As well as can be expected. She's tough." Tougher than anyone he knew. And if he could go back in time, build a time machine and make things right, he would.

"I'm glad to hear that. You guys back together now?"

"Yes," Evan said, even though he and Isla weren't. He wanted the world to think they were together again because he wanted whoever was after her to know she was protected. And that anyone wanting to hurt her would have to go through him to get to her. Ollie was a decent guy, but Evan figured he would still tell people at work about him and Isla. He wanted word to spread fast. "Now what did you find?"

"Someone hacked into the system using a security protocol that didn't get updated. I've since fixed it and ensured that it won't happen again. Some of the team and I are going to go through all these feeds one by one, so it's a little time-consuming. Once we're done we should be able to trace whoever hacked it back to their IP."

He didn't like it, but it explained the loops he'd been looking at. "Have you told the police?"

"Not yet. I've got to tell Isla first and then see what she says—though I imagine it will be to inform the cops. Regardless, I don't have anything solid to give them yet and I'd rather go to them with evidence first. And I can move a hell of a lot faster than their guys anyway." There was a touch of arrogance in his tone, but Evan figured it was earned, considering how many degrees the guy had.

"Good. I'll let Isla know, but I'm sure she'll want to talk to you. Keep me in the loop," he said, even though he had absolutely no authority over Ollie. He didn't think the guy was going to question him now though.

"Will do."

Once they disconnected, Evan rubbed a hand over his face. Well...someone had hacked the security system. Which was bad, but it meant they had a way to track the guy.

He glanced up as Isla stepped into his office, completely dressed for work. She had on a dark gray pencil skirt—one that was very familiar. About a month before the bombing he distinctly remembered shoving that one up to her waist right before they'd made love on his office couch. He resisted the impulse to look over at the seating area, hating the distance between them now. He had so many memories of her here—everywhere.

She was so close, just feet away, but still out of reach. He wanted to erase the past, make things how they used to be, but he didn't know how—and didn't think it was possible.

He shook the thoughts away. "Just got off the phone with Ollie. Your system was hacked and someone was able to loop feeds around your office so there's no way to see who put that cookie there. He's trying to track down who did it. Thinks he and the team will be able to do it quickly."

"That's great. Why didn't he call me?"

"I think he planned to. But I called him about something I saw on your security feed, and he told me what he'd found. Said he planned to talk to you about it yesterday but then..." He didn't need to spell it out; she knew exactly why Ollie hadn't told her.

She rubbed a hand over her face.

"I'm not trying to step on your toes by reaching out to your security team. I just want to find out who hurt you." He had to shove back the anger rising to the surface. That rage wouldn't do him any good. Catching the bastard and protecting Isla was all that mattered.

"I know you're not. I'm glad you talked to him. I'm just trying to digest everything you told me." She lifted a hand to her throat—where she had faint bruising—before quickly dropping it. She cleared her throat. "You ready to go?"

Nodding, he closed his laptop and stood. He hated the sight of her bruising—actually, he hated who had caused it. But he kept his emotions in check because he didn't want to upset her. They were going to figure out who'd done this. Now that her security team had discovered what was going on, he didn't need to review the feeds any longer. "Yep. What have you got on the agenda this morning?"

"A couple video conference calls I have to take care of, and meetings. Always meetings," she sighed.

"I don't like that you're going in at all," he muttered.

She gave him a pointed look because they'd already had this conversation.

He rounded his desk. "Look, since I'm going to be at your office today, if you have time, let's start outlining some details of the Cooper merger I started with your dad." So far he'd been putting all of the details off on his assistant but if he and Isla started working on it, they could wrap things up fairly quickly.

Her green eyes flared in surprise. "Seriously?"

It was clear why she was surprised—he'd been letting his assistant act as the middleman the last month, to keep space between him and Isla, and that had slowed things down. He didn't want space between them anymore. "No more middleman. You and I can wrap things up by the end of the year." Relief flickered across her face and once again he felt like an asshole for how he'd handled things before. "Look, I need to tell you something…" He picked up his tablet from his desk and strode over to her, holding it out.

Her eyebrows drew tighter together as she scanned, scrolling down the touchscreen with her finger. "What the heck is all this? Why on earth would someone print this when it's patently false? It's just going to open them up to liability, even if it is a garbage gossip rag." Frown deepening, she passed the tablet back to him.

"I leaked the story. I confirmed everything."

She blinked. "You told this reporter that we're back together and heading toward an engagement!" Now she was all anger and she had every right to be.

"Not the engagement stuff. I just 'confirmed' that we were a couple again. After what happened, I'm not leaving your side. I'm not letting you get hurt again." He'd kill anyone who came after her. He was still angry with himself for the way he'd treated her, and if someone actually tried to hurt her too? God help them.

"You should've asked me first."

"Yeah, probably."

"No, definitely." Her mouth tightened and he knew he'd screwed up.

Hell, he'd known it when he'd done it, but he hadn't wanted to take the chance she'd say no. Whoever was out there needed to think twice before coming after her

again and he'd rather be a target than her. He could handle himself, and he would. Maybe he should change tac-
tics though, appeal to her business sense.

"Look, once this story spreads it will also solidify our
upcoming deal. Everyone involved will be more secure
if the two biggest partners are together romantically.
We certainly aren't going to sell each other out." It was
archaic but true.

"You just have everything figured out, don't you?"
There was a sharp snap to her tone.

"Not hardly." He didn't have her figured out at all, or
know what to do to win her back. "But this is for the
best."

She muttered something under her breath he couldn't
quite make out, which was probably a good thing.

"Isla, I'm sorry. So damn sorry."

Ignoring his apology, she straightened and lifted her
purse onto her shoulder. "I have a lot of work to do. I'm
ready to leave."

"Once the police bring down your stalker or whoever
this guy is, I'll leak another story that you ended things
with me." It twisted his guts to say it.

Her spine straightened even more, her eyes flashing.
"You think that's why I'm angry? How about you let me
make some decisions where all of this is concerned? This
is my life, and you've just barged in and taken over. Not
to mention this could make you a target too! You've
probably just put yourself in danger, because whoever
this guy is won't have a problem going after my 'boy-
friend.'"

"I know."

She stalked toward him, her heels making soft little sounds over the throw rug. "What do you mean?"

"I mean, I *know* I might be a target. Better me than you."

"You make me crazy! But...you're making it really hard to be mad at you." Then she gave him an unreadable look as she turned back around—giving him a nice shot of her perfect ass.

Grunting, he didn't respond one way or another as he picked up his things.

He had a lot to make up for but he wasn't sorry for this. Because no matter what, she was his to protect. He simply couldn't turn off the part of himself driving him to keep her safe.

# CHAPTER FOURTEEN

"So tell me what you've got—in layman's terms," Isla said as she stood next to Ollie's chair, eyeing the bank of computer screens in front of them.

"Like I told Evan, someone hacked into the security system using a backdoor. I've completely closed up the loop but I'm in the process of going through all of our old feeds. The whole team is. I'm going to see if I can discover if any of the original feeds were saved somewhere or if they were erased..."

Isla's eyes started to glaze over as he explained things to her. She understood the gist of what he was saying at least, but half of it she had no clue about. When he was done, she said, "So basically someone hacked in, took over the feeds and made us see old loops instead of what was actually going on."

"Yes. And whoever did it is very smart," he muttered, annoyance in his voice. "We only caught this because of the audit."

"Is this an inside job?" That worried her.

"It's too soon to tell. And I don't want to speculate either way."

That wasn't a no. "Can you tell when it happened exactly? How long they've had access to our feeds and how extensive the hacking was?"

"Barely a month ago, and it was restricted to a few of our cameras. And the security is on a separate server from everything else. So nothing else has been touched. No files, nothing. It's very localized and it doesn't appear as if any of our contracts or anything else important were touched or compromised."

She breathed a small sigh of relief. "That's something at least. Thanks." She planned to have an outside security firm rip everything apart—because she was not happy this had happened in the first place—but she kept that to herself. "Can you look into all of Rodney Wood's files and email communication before he was fired?"

"Sure. Anything in particular I'm looking for?"

"Anything that might be useful, that might point to him having a personal issue with me or anyone at the company."

He swiveled in his chair to face her. Pushing his slightly too long blond hair back out of his face, he shook his head. "No problem. Anything else?"

"I know all his badges were deactivated when he was fired, but...dig deep." Rodney fit the height for the man who had attacked her and he was the most recent firing—and the circumstances had been bad. She had to go with her instinct on this. "And this is a priority."

"You got it, boss."

"Soon I won't be your boss," she said, smiling faintly. He was moving on to a startup and had told her that he was looking forward to using his degrees more. He did a lot for her company but she could understand wanting to flex his mental muscles. She certainly wanted out of this corporate atmosphere, although for a different reason.

"Yeah, it'll be weird, but I'm excited."

"Good. Just know that if you ever change your mind, you'll have a home here."

"Thanks. I'm hoping this change fits... And I'll be able to wear T-shirts and jeans every day," he said, laughing as he leaned back in his chair, slightly flexing his arm muscles as he stretched. His button-down shirt was shoved up to his forearms, his jacket hung over his chair and she'd seen his tie shoved into one of the pockets. While his clothes weren't ill-fitting, he'd never seemed comfortable in the formal gear.

She wished she didn't have to wear such formal corporate attire either—then reminded herself that after these deals were closed, she'd be moving on too. No more skirts and uncomfortable heels for her either.

Just then Logan stepped into the security room, but he was on his cell phone. Tall with dark hair and a little scruff on his face, he had on a suit—complete with his shirt, tie and jacket all neatly in place. Now *he* looked like the epitome of a security guy who took his job seriously. They nodded at each other before he sat down in front of his work area, continuing to talk to whoever was on the other line.

"Well, you know where to find me," she said to Ollie, heading to the door. "I'll be here most of the day in meetings but if you find out anything, I want to know immediately. Especially concerning Rodney—or whoever."

As she stepped out of the office, she found Madeleine walking down the hallway, looking at her tablet and frowning. Her heels clicked against the newly installed luxury vinyl tile.

"What's up?" Isla asked as she shut the door to the security room behind her.

Madeleine blinked as she looked up. "What? Oh, our PR department just alerted me that someone left some horrible reviews about us on Glassdoor. One right after the other. They're very clearly bogus and I have a feeling I know who left them." She turned her tablet around for Isla to see.

As she read the garbage reviews, she frowned. She didn't micromanage and there was no way for her to know every single thing about the company, but the majority of these complaints were definitely bogus. They had great health care, competitive benefits and annual bonuses on top of higher than industry average raises. Though according to these reviews, none of that was true.

"I think this is Rodney."

*Ugh.* "Well, I've got security looking into all of his files and emails, doing a detailed comb-through."

"I wouldn't be surprised if he found a way to bypass security," Madeleine muttered. "He'd been here long enough. I just don't like any of this, especially what happened to you."

Her either. "Let Logan or Ollie know about these reviews too. See if they can find any similar syntax in any of his emails. It might help if we have that kind of information when we hand things over to the police."

"Good thinking."

She was very motivated right now. More than anyone, she wanted to find out who wanted her dead. And she hated that she hadn't gotten a clear view of her attacker. Everything had happened so quickly and she'd been so concerned with getting away that she hadn't retained any details. Other than the man had been wearing a hoodie and had been fairly tall.

*Super helpful,* she thought, annoyed at herself.

The other images that flashed through her mind were the bright fluorescent light overhead, the way the vending machine had rattled as she'd slammed into it, the overwhelming sanitary scent—and the subtle underlying cologne of her attacker. Or maybe it had been laundry detergent.

Phantom pain flared in her neck as she remembered the feel of his arm wrapped around her throat, but she quickly murmured a goodbye and headed back to her floor. She knew she would have to mentally deal with her ordeal later, but she was putting a bandage over it for now and hoping it stuck in place.

\* \* \*

Isla paused as she strode past the bay of windows of the conference room where Evan was working. After what had happened yesterday, he'd informed her that he would be working out of her building and sticking close to her instead of going into his own office.

She'd never been so simultaneously angry and touched by someone. It didn't matter that he'd apologized for leaking that stupid story. She was still hurt by what he'd done—and pissed that he'd put himself in danger. The man made her crazy, but that was the last thing she wanted. He'd been through enough and now he was basically painting a target on himself by linking himself to her. It was maddening to say the least.

She was trying to let her anger go, she really was. But the fact that he'd made such a big decision and just decided to tell some random journalist that they were back together brought up a whole lot of feelings she was trying to keep buried. At least for the near future. But...she also understood he was trying to protect her, which was sweet if misguided. So, in short, her emotions were all over the place and he was to blame.

When he glanced up from his laptop and made eye contact, she couldn't pretend she hadn't seen him. As he waved her inside, she inwardly winced. She wasn't sure she was ready to deal with Evan right now. Thankfully he wasn't following her around to every meeting and office she visited but that was only because she'd fought him on that—and because the building was basically in lockdown today with security hyperalert.

"Hey, what's up?" she asked, pushing the glass door open.

"I've got us a meeting with Nic Bentley tonight if you can swing it. He's having a cocktail party but I think we can close the Cooper merger a lot faster than anticipated since he's agreed to meet us. The groundwork is already there because of..." His expression shuttered and she knew what he'd been about to say.

Her father and Evan had already laid all the groundwork before the explosion that had ruined so many lives. But she did *not* have time to get emotional today so she brushed past it. "That's great. You sure Bentley is ready to meet? Last I talked to his assistant, he was still blowing me off."

"I'm sure."

"Good." Evan really did have the golden touch. Just not with her anymore. "Listen, I spoke to Ollie and he explained what he's found. I'm also having him dig more into Rodney Wood's emails. I think Rodney also might've left some bogus Glassdoor reviews trashing the company. Which, considering how many great ones we have, I'm not worried about it. But I am worried about *him.*"

"You think he might be the one behind the texts and your attack?"

"Honestly, I don't know. We've had a few run-ins, and he wasn't very respectful of me or other women in general, it seems. Which is part of the reason he was fired. At this point he's the only person I can really think of with that kind of hostility toward me. Plus he was *just* fired so the timing works. If he was going to go postal, it would be right after he was let go, right? I'm sure I could have other enemies, but I just can't think of anyone. So I figured we should go with the obvious, the person who sticks out."

"Have you told Detective Duarte about him?"

"I gave his name and all the info I had to him so it's probable that he's either brought him in or plans to. But if security finds anything from mining his emails, I'll forward that along as well. Hey…if you were going to do an outside audit of your security system, who would you use?"

"Red Stone, and not just because I trust Lizzy. They've got a small division that handles that sort of thing. It's headed up by a crew with excellent credentials—Lizzy included. Pretty sure a couple of them used to be spies. Not her though."

"Wow, okay then. The breach with our security never should have happened. I haven't said anything to the team, but I'm going to bring in an outsider to make sure everything is truly secure. I'm not sure how angry I should be about this breach yet." Since that wasn't her area of expertise, she didn't know if this truly had been an unavoidable mistake or if someone had dropped the ball. Her father would have known. And this was a reminder that while she could handle a lot of day-to-day things, she was out of her depth with the security angle.

"Good. It's what I would do too. And…it doesn't hurt to do security reviews annually regardless."

"Thanks for the recommendation. Do you need me for anything?" she asked.

"No. I have a video conference call set up. So when does Geno get here?" His question was casual but his shoulders immediately tightened.

She knew he didn't want her going anywhere, and after what had happened she wasn't planning on leaving the building. Anyone who wanted access to this floor had to be scanned and approved. Unfortunately for him, Geno was on that list.

Security was ramped up today and she was sticking to meetings that were preset. "In the next hour. We should be finalizing everything today. Mostly anyway. Soon enough, everyone will sign on the dotted line if our lawyers can agree."

"Do you want me in the meeting with you?"

She lifted an eyebrow. "Ha, ha. There's no way Geno is behind any of this. If he was, I wouldn't be working with him. I'm not afraid to be alone with him. You just don't like him."

Evan lifted a shoulder, not bothering to deny it. "Did he ever ask you out?"

She blinked and cleared her throat. "I'm not sure how that matters."

All that tension ratcheted up as he shifted in his seat, his big body tense. "So that's a yes."

Oh, she was not discussing this with him. He'd lost the right to be jealous when he'd shut her out at a time when they'd needed each other most. "Well, you know where I am if you need me." She smiled sweetly and left the conference room. For some reason she kind of liked that Evan was jealous—and then felt crappy for it.

It meant he still cared. And no matter how much she wanted to deny it, she'd never stopped lov— *Nope.* She wasn't going there. She couldn't handle it right now.

They were so close to closing these last few deals, and she was also worried about whatever lunatic out there wanted her dead. She had enough on her plate and could not think about Evan or her stupid feelings right now. Especially since she wasn't even sure where she stood as far as he was concerned.

# CHAPTER FIFTEEN

"You look great." Evan drank in the sight of Isla as she stepped out of her private office bathroom. She'd changed into a simple black sheath dress and had on heels that defined the slim curves of her calves. He flashed back to how many times she'd had those very sexy calves slung over his shoulders as he'd gone down on her. Quickly, he forced himself to think of anything else.

She gave him a ghost of a smile. "Thanks. I'm kind of tired of all these meetings, if I'm being honest. I feel like I don't have a life anymore."

Evan knew Isla hadn't wanted to follow in her father's footsteps, but she'd been so quick to take over everything that he just assumed she'd changed her mind. Clearly that wasn't the case. Over the course of the day it had been obvious that she had no passion for any of this, even if she was good at it. "Why don't you just pass this off to someone else? You don't have to head up your father's previous deals." And he hated that she was taking all this on.

"Intellectually I know that, but there's some part of me that needs to see these deals through. I need to finish them for him."

"Your father wouldn't think any less of you if you farmed them out to your very capable employees. People he personally hired." Douglas McDonald had been vigilant about who he hired, especially senior-level employees.

Her lips curved up slightly. "Maybe. But you know I won't do that."

"Maybe you should." Now he felt like an even bigger ass for dragging his feet on their deal. Even if he'd wanted to avoid seeing her, he should have sucked it up and dealt with everything. "At least with the one you and I are working on, it's mostly done anyway. If you want, let me handle the rest of it. At this point we just need Bentley to sign off and we're good." And Evan could handle that trust-fund jackass.

She paused and he could see that she wanted to say yes, was desperate to. But then she shook her head. "Come on, let's get this meeting over with. I seriously don't understand why Bentley won't meet during regular business hours."

"Because he's a jackass who sleeps in until three in the afternoon." Evan's tone was dry.

Isla let out a startled laugh—a real one, and the first he'd heard from her in ages. "Right? If we didn't need him so badly, I would say let's forget tonight, and forget him. At least a cocktail party doesn't sound so bad."

Smiling, he picked up Isla's jacket for her and started to wrap his arm around her shoulders as they stepped out of her office, but stopped himself at the last second.

Bentley's father had died in the same bombing that had killed Isla's dad and injured Evan—and subsequently Bentley had been given a multimillion-dollar business.

Now Nic Bentley had more shares than any of the board, so they couldn't get rid of him. Evan couldn't imagine what his father had been thinking, leaving everything to the irresponsible partier. Nicolas Senior had wanted to give his son responsibility, but the older man had enabled the asshole son his entire life, so Evan wasn't sure why Bentley Senior would expect him to change now.

Now Bentley Junior was running his business into the ground even more, and Evan and Isla wanted to scoop it up while it was still profitable and save thousands of jobs. But time was ticking because their investors would only hold on for so long. Really good people were already jumping ship, making things even more difficult.

"We should be able to get in and out of there quickly enough and gauge whether he's truly interested in this deal or not," Isla said. "If he's not... How do you feel about walking away?" Her tone was hesitant and he figured he knew why.

The original deal was the last one Evan had worked on with Douglas, the one left unfinished. "I'm okay with it. He needs us way more than we need this business." Evan didn't want to walk away, but he also didn't want Isla to work herself to death.

She needed to put the past behind her—they both did. If that meant this deal didn't go through...so be it. Isla's happiness was worth more to him than any amount of money ever could be.

\* \* \*

Thirty minutes later, Isla glanced over at Evan. "Can you believe this crap?" she asked as he steered down the residential street teeming with traffic. Red and purple spotlights flashed around the house and up into the sky as if this was Universal or Disney. It was ridiculous. So much for this just being a cocktail party.

At least a hundred cars were parked in front of the mansion, scattered all over the expansive property. The thump of music was audible in the distance and she had no doubt it was coming from the party. Man, she bet Bentley's neighbors hated him.

"Unfortunately yes. We should just leave," he muttered.

She eyed the wide-open gates as Evan drove past. "Are we really leaving?"

"I have a friend who lives a few houses down. We're going to park there. I don't want to risk my car getting blocked in. Because this is clearly a shitshow."

"Oh, good idea." She didn't like being out at all, but Detective Duarte had given her a courtesy call and told her they were fairly certain that Rodney was behind the poisoning and hospital attack on her. He couldn't tell her more or why he thought that, but he'd wanted to give her peace of mind when he'd let her know that Rodney was currently being questioned by the police. He'd asked for an attorney, but at least he was in custody. It made her feel better about being out tonight. "Are you sure you don't want to leave?" This party had nightmare written all over it.

"I want to say yes, but with Rodney in police custody we should be fine. And I'm carrying." He patted his jacket once and she knew he had a gun under there. It wasn't like he always had a weapon on him, but right now she was grateful that he did. "Let's get in and out. If Bentley is too hammered to talk to us, we'll leave. I know a way to strong-arm him into meeting with us." His tone was positively savage.

Isla shot him a surprised look. "Seriously?"

"Yes. I'm not proud of it but...I can make a meeting with us happen. I just didn't want to go that route. I want everything to go as smoothly as possible where this deal is concerned. It matters."

She nodded because she understood. It did matter. Evan had been right earlier when he'd called her out for working on these deals when she didn't necessarily need to. There were plenty of capable people who worked at her father's company. Her company. *Damn it.* She couldn't quite think of it as her own. Probably never would. But some part of her—that little girl who still needed her father's approval—didn't want to disappoint her dad or dishonor his legacy. So here she was, working stupid hours at a stupid party, meeting a frat-boy man-baby who'd never grown up so she could help close her father's final deal.

"Hey," Evan murmured, reaching his hand out to hers as he turned into a quiet, gated driveway. "We can leave."

"No, I...I was just thinking about my dad."

He paused as he pulled up to the gate and let the security know he was there to park—he must have texted his friend, or they knew who Evan was. She was betting on the latter.

As the gate opened for them, he squeezed her hand once. "I think about him a lot. I'll find myself wanting to call him over random things and then it hits me that I can't. And I know it's got to be harder for you, especially since you've stepped into his shoes so seamlessly."

"It is, thanks. I'm reminded of him every day. It's why I didn't take his old office. I just couldn't stomach the thought of sitting at his desk, of truly taking over." And that was about all she could say on that. She didn't want to start talking about her dad or she'd get emotional. Right now, that wasn't what she wanted. She simply wanted to talk to Bentley and then get out of here and back home.

Well, not home, but Evan's place, since she was still staying there for the time being. Which was a whole other can of worms she was dealing with. She'd slept in his bed last night and she couldn't deny the attraction she still had for him. The man was under her skin, in her soul and she... She didn't know if she could let go of things and move on. Though she wanted to, for both their sakes.

"I ordered you a box of that biscotti you love," he said as he steered down the driveway, slowing when they reached a parking section off to the right of the four-car garage.

Her heart rate kicked up. "Seriously?" She'd searched online and hadn't been able to find the supplier.

"Yep. I figured after what happened, you deserved that damn biscotti."

"I kind of want to kiss you right now," she blurted, then pulled her hand from his and started to laugh it off, to tell him that she didn't mean that, but couldn't force the lie out. Because the truth was, she was crazy enough to want to kiss Evan Bishop. Now and all the time. The man owned her heart whether she wanted it or not. She couldn't escape her feelings, and it was that much harder now that they were sleeping under the same roof.

"I wouldn't stop you if you did." His words were as heated as his expression.

*Oh, no. Nope. Not happening.* Instead of responding, like a coward she escaped the now parked car, grabbing her small purse before shutting the door behind her.

"So...we're not going to discuss that?" he asked as he rounded the vehicle.

She glanced away from him and focused on the flashing lights half a street down. "Nope."

He didn't comment, just linked his arm through hers as they started walking along the driveway.

Being so close to him like this was familiar in a way that made her ache. His scent wrapped around her, teasing her, making her think about how easy it would be to simply kiss him, to give in to her impulses. But then where would they be? If they kissed, it would definitely lead to more. But what the hell could he offer her? And once this mess with Rodney was over, he could back out of her life just like before.

Sure, he'd told her that he just wanted to be friends, but she didn't know how that was possible. Not for her anyway. And she wasn't sure how it was possible for him either. Because he was jealous of Geno, a man she had no real relationship with, other than a working one. What happened when one of them started dating?

*Ugh. No way.* She couldn't even think about him with another woman. It would bring on a wave of sadness, and she simply could not deal with that right now.

CHAPTER SIXTEEN

He stared across the crowd of scantily clad people, surprised that Isla and Evan were here. And going by the way Evan had his arm draped around her shoulders possessively, keeping her close, it was clear they were together. As in *truly* together.

This wasn't some publicity stunt as he'd thought it might be.

Glaring at the two of them, he grabbed a drink from a passing server and tossed back what turned out to be vodka. It burned going down so he grabbed another.

Why was she here tonight, throwing her relationship with Bishop in his face?

It was as if she was taunting him, mocking him. He loved her, but maybe she was like all the others. Just a whore. Otherwise why would she go back to Bishop? A man who didn't love her, didn't respect her. No, she was just like all the other women he'd been with—and there were many.

He gritted his teeth, shaking off the touch of a random woman who started stroking his forearm and asking if he wanted to dance. He turned away, needing distance from Isla and Bishop before he did something stupid.

He made his way through the crowd and grabbed another drink as he stalked around the pool, making his way inside.

He'd planned on having fun tonight—and finding a thin redhead who looked enough like Isla to fuck—but seeing her with Bishop had ruined everything. For so long, he'd wanted only her, even when he'd been with other women, even his ex. But now...things seemed clearer.

He was a fool with a fool's dream. Apparently she just liked being with a man who treated her like garbage, who disposed of her as if she didn't matter—but she came running when Bishop called. He gritted his teeth, barely noticing his surroundings as he moved. If he couldn't have her, Bishop sure wasn't going to. That man didn't deserve her.

He shoved a waiter out of the way, ignoring the man's cry of surprise as he stalked inside. He needed to cool off, to take a few deep breaths and collect himself before he left the party.

He couldn't stay another moment. Not when she was here with Bishop.

He'd been keeping an eye on her for so long, waiting until the time was right to make his move. Maybe that was the problem. He needed to stop waiting, to stop being such a pussy.

He needed to take what he deserved—her.

CHAPTER SEVENTEEN

Isla was tired of waiting for the bathroom but she'd had far too much water tonight. The line was ridiculous, and considering the size of this party? She couldn't believe Bentley didn't have better facilities.

Annoyed that Bentley had blown her and Evan off a few times—and just frustrated in general that she was here on a weekday night—she leaned against the hallway wall, trying to find some relief for her tired feet. This was what she got for wearing stupid heels.

When she shifted slightly to look for Evan, who'd insisted on waiting at the end of the hallway for her, she nearly jerked back when she saw some woman trying to drape herself all over him.

Gritting her teeth, she rolled her shoulders once. She and Evan weren't together. She didn't have any claim on him. Except she kind of did since they were in a fake relationship right now, and the least he could do was fake it and push the woman off him.

She peeked around the person in front of her again and saw that the woman leaning toward Evan hadn't stepped back any. No, she was all up in his personal space.

Temper spiking, Isla slipped out of line and turned the other way. She knew where another bathroom was and she was going to take care of business, then they

154 | KATIE REUS

were getting the hell out of here. She could tell that Evan was annoyed with the woman by the tense line of his jaw and his tight body language, but still, she wasn't going to stand here for the next fifteen minutes and watch that woman throw herself at him. Isla had limits and that was one of them. She'd never had insecurities where Evan was concerned, but now? After the way he'd shut her out for so long, it seemed she had more than she imagined.

She took a left at the end of the hallway and made her way to the front of the house. Two sets of stairs arched upward in a beautiful sweep. She'd been here before, on two occasions, both with her father for some boring dinner party. The first time she'd received a tour, so she knew there was a nice little half bath right at the top of the stairs.

With no line. She hurried up the stairs, figuring she'd be done before Evan even knew she was gone.

Once she was done, she splashed water on her face and gave herself a hard look in the mirror. She wasn't so sure she liked what she saw. She kept telling herself that as soon as these deals were done, she was moving on and would do everything she'd been dreaming of.

*Planning on.*

She'd already talked to Marcy about expanding the community center and building another one on the opposite side of town—because there weren't nearly enough federally funded places for kids. Not good ones, anyway. She'd even spoken to Dylan Blackwood about properties and he had a few lined up for her to look at. But...deep down she wondered if she was dragging her feet because she was afraid she would fail. Which was stupid. Because if she did nothing, she was failing anyway.

"Stop second-guessing yourself," she muttered. Then frowned. "And stop talking to yourself."

Stepping out of the bathroom, she finger-combed her hair and headed for the stairs. As she reached the top, she turned at a whisper of sound behind her. Clothes or something rustling. She wasn't sure what it was, but suddenly she wasn't alone.

A man stood in the shadows, his big body vibrating with menace.

Panic punched through her and she felt like she was in the hospital all over again. Turning, she grasped the railing of the stairs and started to hurry down. As she moved, her heels slipped and she launched forward, unable to stop herself from tumbling. She cried out as her elbow and knee banged against the rug runner.

"Oh my God, are you okay?" A man wearing black pants and a black long-sleeved shirt with a small name-tag on the right pocket raced up the bottom half of the stairs. He was part of the subtle security team Bentley had hired.

Groaning, she let him help her up. Glancing over her shoulder, she looked back upstairs as he helped her to her feet, but didn't see anyone there.

Jesus, had she imagined the whole thing? No, there had been someone up there, but it wasn't as if the man had said anything, or taken even a step in her direction.

156 | KATIE REUS

She'd simply gotten spooked and then nearly taken a header down the stairs. It was time to go.

Damn it, she never should have come tonight at all. At least no one was in the foyer to see her limping along. Even so, her face burned with embarrassment. If anyone had witnessed that, they'd assume she was drunk and it would make it into a gossip section online.

She still hadn't dealt with her attack, and being here was clearly messing with her head, making her imagine menacing men in the dark. She knew she needed to emotionally handle what had happened, and she'd been hoping that throwing herself into work would help. But being here after what had happened yesterday—she realized it was way too soon. She was trying to take on too much.

"Your dress is ripped," the man said as he slid an arm around her waist, helping her walk down the rest of the stairs.

Wincing, she looked down and saw that yep, the hem of her dress was ripped. Pain ricocheted through her knee and elbow, her body sore as they reached the bottom of the stairs. Oh yeah, coming tonight had clearly been a dumb idea.

"Is there a private room I can sit in for a moment?" she asked, reaching into her purse to call Evan.

"Of course, this way."

As they headed down another hallway, in the opposite direction of the raging party, they ran into Geno.

She wasn't sure who was more surprised—her or him. "Geno, I didn't know you were going to be here." He looked a little rumpled, his shirt wrinkled and his hair mussed.

"Are you okay?" he asked, taking in her ripped dress. Just as quickly his gaze narrowed on the security guy. "What the hell happened!"

"Nothing. I'm just clumsy, that's all," she said, not wanting to get into it.

Geno opened the nearest door before the security guy could but the man with the nametag that said Mark didn't argue, simply walked in with them.

"Here." Geno slid off his jacket and put it around her shoulders. "Now tell me what happened."

"Nothing. And I'm fine, I swear. Just embarrassed at my clumsiness."

"Get her an ice pack," Geno snapped out, his tone so forceful that Mark pretty much jumped up and raced from the room.

"Thank you," she said quietly as she pulled out her phone and quickly texted Evan. She knew she should probably call him but she also knew he was going to be seriously annoyed with her for disappearing like that. And she was putting off talking to him until the last minute possible. "You don't need to stay with me. Seriously. I just took a tumble down half the stairs because I apparently forgot how to walk in heels."

Before he could respond, Evan strode through the open doorway, his eyes narrowing as he focused on Geno. It was clear he wanted to say something to the other man, but instead he hurried over to Isla and knelt in front of her. "Are you okay? What happened?"

"I'm clumsy."

He narrowed his gaze again and she found herself unable to look away from him. That was how it had always been. This man had stolen her heart, and no matter how much she would like to deny it, he still owned it. If he stepped into a room, her eyes were on him, no one else. No way around it.

"No you're not." His voice was dry.

Sighing, she looked away, embarrassed. "I was coming down the stairs—"

"Why were you upstairs?" he demanded. "You just disappeared."

Her cheeks heated up because she didn't want to have this conversation in front of Geno. Or at all. "I was using the upstairs bathroom because I got sick of waiting in that line. When I got to the top of the stairs, I saw someone and it made me flash back to what happened at the hospital. Some fight or flight instinct kicked in and I panicked. No one attacked me or anything, I just...I got scared. Apparently I'm not handling things as well as I thought I was," she whispered.

His eyes softened just a bit. "I knew we shouldn't have come here tonight. We're leaving." He stood, all his muscles tight.

"You can't wait for her to get some ice?" Geno stepped forward, his jaw clenched hard. "She just fell down the damn stairs!"

Evan swiveled and stood, the two men facing off with each other as if they planned to come to blows.

"Stop," she said quietly. "Whatever the heck is happening between you two, just stop. We're going to wait for ice because my knee hurts, and then we're leaving." Even though Evan's shoulders were tense, he eased back from his aggressive stance.

Thankfully Mark returned with a bag of ice and a bottle of water for her. "I've let Mr. Bentley know what happened and he's very sorry. He's getting out of the pool and has said he'd like to talk to you—"

"I appreciate it, but it's fine." She and Evan had been trying to get the man alone for the last two hours and she was done waiting. She took the ice, thanked Mark, then looked at Geno. "We're still on for tomorrow?"

"Are you kidding me?" Evan helped her to her feet. "You've taken on too much. Now isn't the time for work."

Something inside her snapped. "I'll work all I want! I need this deal done so I can pass the company on. I'm done with my father's business. I'm done with everything. As soon as these deals are completed, I'm selling the company." The words were out in a whirlwind and she belatedly realized she shouldn't have let such big information drop in front of Geno, but what was done was done.

Evan stilled, staring for a long second. To her surprise, he didn't respond, simply slid Geno's jacket off her shoulders, and instead of handing it to the other man, dumped it on the couch. "Thank you for being here for Isla," he said coldly. Then he slid off his own jacket and wrapped it around her, his possessiveness clear as he helped her to the door.

"I'll call you tomorrow," she murmured to Geno, ignoring Evan's growl of annoyance as they silently left the room.

She'd just dropped a bomb and there was nothing really to say.

Of course now that they were headed back to his place she knew Evan would want to talk about what she'd just said. Under different circumstances, she would be leaning on him.

Just like she used to. But the past was over. There was no more "them."

And damn it, she needed to get on board with that. Her head could, but her heart was another matter.

# CHAPTER EIGHTEEN

"Would you please say something?" Isla asked as they stepped into Evan's condo. Residual aches lingered throughout her body but she knew it wouldn't last long. Or she hoped not. She couldn't take much more.

He shut the door with more force than necessary and clicked the lock into place. "I just can't believe you left like that." She could tell he was trying to rein in his anger—but he wasn't doing a great job of it.

"I didn't leave. I was just finding another—"

"I know what you said. It's bullshit. I don't even know how you snuck away," he muttered.

"The man the police suspect of attacking me is in custody. I wasn't in any danger. And I didn't feel like watching that woman hanging all over you! Maybe you should have been paying more attention." She shouted the last part, surprising herself and him if his stunned expression was any indication. She wasn't a yeller, never had been. But he was bringing it all out right now.

He blinked, straightening, his entire body language changing. "What woman?"

"You know very well who I'm talking about."

He stared at her for a long moment and then she saw when it clicked into place. "Sabrina? She's friends with my family and I've never been with her."

"I'm very aware of that fact."

"Then what the hell?"

"I guess I got jealous," she muttered.

Now he stared at her in pure shock. "Why on earth would you be jealous of her? Of anyone?"

"Because I have no claim on you!" she shouted, the words tumbling from her. "This stupid fake relationship is just that. Fake. And when Rodney is arrested, we'll go back to like it was before." Only it would be worse. Because she'd gotten a taste of him in her life again and now she wanted more.

He stepped closer, invading her personal space, his masculine scent wrapping around her. "First of all, you have *every* claim on me," he growled, looking down at her as if he wanted to kiss her senseless.

And she was definitely going to let him if he tried. "Is there a second of all?"

"Yes." He cupped her cheek, giving her plenty of time to pull away.

When she didn't move, his mouth was on hers in an instant, soft and gentle, his tongue teasing hers, giving and taking. She moaned, leaning into him as if pulled by a magnet.

But he pulled back, frowning down at her. "I don't want to hurt you. We need to get more ice—"

She grabbed his shirt and yanked him down to her. She was sore, but she was fine. More than fine if she got him in the process.

As she tasted him, she savored every second of their kiss, of the way he made her feel desirable and wanted.

The sensation of being in his arms again was too much and yet not enough. She wanted more than kisses.

He groaned into her mouth, cupping her cheek again as he gently backed her up against the nearest wall. She arched into him, her breasts rubbing against his chest as she debated if she should start stripping both of them here or wait until they were in his bedroom. When he'd said she had every claim on him, something inside her had shifted.

Breathing hard, he tore his mouth from hers. "I don't want to do this if you're going to regret it." It looked as if it took every ounce of energy he had to get those words out.

"I don't want to stop." Maybe she'd regret it, but she didn't think so. She was going to own her decisions. She wanted Evan Bishop. At least physically. She'd figure everything else out later.

He placed a hand on the wall next to her head, his eyes flashing with hunger. "Stay in my room tonight. Don't walk out on me after we... If we..."

"I'm not going anywhere." She reached for him again at the same time he reached for her.

She wasn't sure what she was thinking, what they were thinking. Except that she desperately needed him— wanted him. She wasn't sure how much he was capable of giving her or how much she was capable of letting go.

But right now she needed him like she needed her next breath.

Impatient and desperate for Isla, Evan lifted her up and carried her the rest of the way to his bedroom. The other night up against the wall of that cold, impersonal condo hadn't felt right. It had been hot, and she'd climaxed, but it hadn't been them. It had just been like the condo itself—there had been no warmth, connection or intimacy. And it had barely taken the edge off.

Now, he wanted to take his time with her. To pleasure her, to hear her cry out his name as she came against his mouth and around his cock.

The hallway passed by in a blur as he hungrily kissed her and carried her to his bedroom. She was holding on to him as if she was afraid he'd change his mind. *Not in a million years.*

The floor-to-ceiling automatic shades were still up, letting in the outside lights from downtown, illuminating the bed more than enough.

He didn't bother moving the covers as he stretched her out in front of him. God, he'd missed her. Missed her so damn much. He ached with the knowledge that it was his fault they hadn't spoken or seen each other for two months. Two long, torturous months. He needed to make it up to her. Show her how badly he still hungered for her.

"You okay?" He gently slipped her heels off. He couldn't believe his hands actually shook, but hell, this was Isla. He was desperate for her with an intensity that floored him. Always had been. And nothing had changed.

She propped up on her elbows, watching him intently. "I need you."

Well if that wasn't what he needed to hear, he didn't know what was. Looking at her now, he couldn't believe he'd ever been stupid enough to try to cut her out of his life. But guilt was a funny thing.

"Undress for me?" Her green eyes filled with too many emotions as she watched him, her gaze hungry, needy.

He shook his head because he wasn't there yet. Hell, he wasn't sure if he would ever be. He had never thought of himself as a vain person, but...

He simply wasn't ready for her to see his scars. He was having a hard enough time dealing with the change.

Instead of pushing him, she sat up on her knees and took off her dress in a few quick motions. The material swooshed quietly as she drew it over her head and tossed it aside.

He sucked in a breath to see her almost completely bare for him, the thin little wisps of material covering her breasts and pussy. She'd always liked lacy little things—and he loved seeing them on her.

"Lie back," he demanded as he crawled onto the bed.

She did as he ordered, stretching out, a sensual look on her face. He crawled up her body, feathering kisses over her calves, the shallow little scrapes on her knees where she'd fallen, her inner thighs, teasing his tongue right along the seam where her inner thigh and mound met. But he didn't make a move to take off the rest of her barely-there coverings. Not yet. He wanted to tease her first.

"Evan." She wriggled against the bed, her legs restless as she impatiently grabbed onto his head.

Smiling against her body, he continued kissing upward, taking his time to savor her. Though he had her body memorized, he still wanted to taste all of her, to convince himself that this was real.

He'd missed more than just the sex since they'd been apart, but he sure as hell had missed that too. A lot. They'd always fit so damn perfectly together and there'd never been anything she hadn't wanted to try.

When he reached her breasts, he lost some of his control as he reached behind her back and quickly unstrapped her bra.

She shifted underneath him, making impatient little sounds that made him smile against her neck. He raked his teeth against her sensitive skin as she wrapped her arms and legs around his body.

His control slipped as he sought out her mouth, kissing, taking, devouring. She was everything to him and he needed all of her.

All his muscles were pulled taut with need as she clung tight to him, only her thong in his way.

That control slipped even more when she started grinding against him, her fingers digging into his back. Growling against her, he laid a new path of kisses back down her body, taking his time with her breasts, not stopping until her nipples were hard little points and wet from his attention.

"I need you in me," she rasped out.

His cock jerked hard against his zipper. *Fuuuuck.* He needed to be in her too. But he had to taste her first. By the time he made it back between her legs, his hands were shaking again as he tugged off the last barrier between them.

He sucked in a sharp breath before slowly running his tongue up her folds, pleasure surging through him when she jerked against his face.

He loved how reactive she was, how reactive she'd always been.

But somehow this felt different, almost new. It didn't matter that he knew her body and she knew his; tonight was somehow new. A rediscovery. A reconnecting.

And if he wanted to win her back—no more "let's be friends" bullshit—he had to take the right step of winning her over. Of getting her to forgive him.

Giving her a lot of orgasms sounded like a good start. Everything else could wait.

He told himself to work his way up to it, to take his time, but when he started teasing her with his tongue, he realized he couldn't draw it out too long.

He was just as desperate to hear her cries of pleasure as he was sure she was desperate to climax.

Wet and slick for him, her body told him exactly how turned on she was. And if he'd had any doubt, the little cries of pleasure she made each time he licked her told him what she needed.

She speared her hands into his hair as he slid two fingers inside her. She was so damn tight.

Moving them in and out, he focused on her clit with his tongue, adding enough pressure, flicking and teasing that tight little bud over and over as she writhed against his face.

He knew she was about to start climaxing about three seconds before it happened. Her inner walls tightened around his fingers, clenching and milking him. His cock hardened even more as he felt how slick and tight she was. Well too damn bad for him, because this was all about her.

He was still in love with her. Had never fallen out of love with her. And their time apart because of his own cowardice only drove that point home even more. This was where he belonged. In her bed, in her life, with her.

Her hips arched off the bed as her orgasm punched through her, her fingers tightening against his head as she came. Her hips rolled over and over as he drew her pleasure out, wanting to extend it as long as possible.

She let out a satisfied sigh as she collapsed against the covers, and when he looked up the length of her body she gave him a sweet, sensual smile. "That was incredible."

He wanted to tell her that *she* was incredible but the words stuck in his throat. As he looked at her like this with the city lights streaming in, leaving her in a soft glow, her long auburn tresses fanned out everywhere, he wanted to memorize this moment forever.

*I love you*, he thought, though he couldn't get the words out. They stuck in his throat as he watched her. All his muscles were tight in anticipation of more but tonight was just about her. At least that was what he told himself. Maybe if he punished himself enough, it would make up for what he'd done. And if he told her now, there was no guarantee she'd even believe him. He needed to show her that he was serious about sticking around. He needed to be a man of action. Not just words.

So when she reached for the front of his pants, he stilled her hands. "You don't—"

"How about you let me do what I want?" There was a heated gleam in her eyes, impossible to ignore as she pushed at his chest. She didn't insist that he remove his shirt. Instead she shoved him on his back and worked at his pants.

How the hell had he thought he could walk away from her, from *them*? She took his hard length into her mouth.

He groaned as she sucked him deep, and as he threaded his fingers through her long hair he didn't think about much else for a long, long time.

She knew him as well as he knew her, and after they'd both found pleasure again, she curled up next to him on the bed, right where she belonged.

He gathered her close even as he thought it was a weird thing to be in bed with her naked and him half-clothed. "I'm still getting used to my scars," he murmured, the words out before he could stop himself. He continued stroking his fingers down her back and though she didn't move, he knew she wasn't asleep yet.

"Take as long as you need, Evan," she murmured.

He nearly jolted at her words, as if it was just as simple as that.

He tightened his hold on her, wanting to say more but not wanting to ruin the moment. With her curled up against him so sweetly—trustingly—he simply closed his eyes and held her close.

For this night, at least, he was going to pretend things between them were perfect, that they had never changed at all.

# CHAPTER NINETEEN

Evan pushed his chair back as the videoconference
screen went dark, glad the meeting was over because all his focus was on Isla, who was down the hall in
another conference room with Geno, Sara Rodriguez—
who was part of their deal—and their attorneys. He knew
Isla was perfectly safe surrounded by so many people, but
the most primitive part of his brain wanted him to be in
that meeting with her, to watch her, to make sure she
was safe.

Which, yes, he knew made him insane. But logic did
not play into his feelings. And it wasn't as if he'd voiced
what he wanted to anyone. Still, he wanted the meeting
over and he wanted Rodney Wood in jail for good.

"You okay, boss?" Ricardo, his assistant, was working
with him today in the conference room. They had a lot
to catch up on, and while both of them could easily work
remotely, some things were much easier done face-to-
face. And Ricardo didn't mind traveling to Isla's building
for work—not when, according to him, they had the best
food trucks nearby.

"Yeah." He looked down at his laptop and had started
to review contract terms for a recent potential acquisi-
tion when there was a sharp knock on the door.

Glancing over, he saw Sara Rodriguez through the
glass.

172 | KATIE REUS

Surprised, he stood as she entered and nodded politely.

"Hey, Evan," she said, waving for him to sit. "I swear you're always working."

He gave her a ghost of a smile. "You're one to talk."

She lifted a shoulder. "I wanted to talk to you about something, a project that came across my desk this morning. I think we'd be a good fit."

Since he had a pulse on Miami, he had a feeling he knew which one she was talking about, and he agreed. "Set it up with Ricardo."

Sara nodded at Ricardo and they both promised to follow up with each other. They might have murmured more polite things, but all of Evan's attention was on Isla. Or rather the fact that he couldn't see Isla. After Sara left, both attorneys followed down the hallway not long after.

But not Conti or Isla.

He kept his shit together though. Barely.

Isla was a grown-ass woman, and he didn't truly think Geno was the one stalking her. Detective Duarte had already told him they were working on a warrant for Rodney Wood and should have it by tomorrow morning. Unfortunately they hadn't been able to hold him in custody indefinitely after their questioning because that wasn't how things worked. Once they had a warrant, however, they should be able to get everything they needed to make a more solid case and arrest him. The judge they were getting it from was apparently out of town, but would be back in the morning. Until then, the

Miami PD had him under surveillance, which made Evan feel better.

It was also the only thing keeping him from going over there and beating the shit out of Rodney. Because if he was the one who had hurt Isla—and the cops were certain he was, though the evidence was just circumstantial—he was lucky he was breathing. If for some reason he didn't go to jail? Evan didn't even want to think about what he'd do. It didn't matter if he and Isla were together or not, she was his to protect.

He shoved those thoughts aside as Geno strode down the hall, looking at something on his cell phone. The too-handsome man glanced over and nodded politely when he saw Evan. But he didn't pause, just kept going.

*Good.* Evan did not have the capacity to be polite today.

A few moments later, Isla stepped into the room. She wore an all-white pantsuit that had very clearly been tailored for her because it hugged her body to perfection, and she looked, well, incredible. She'd styled her hair into soft curls this morning—in his bathroom—and they framed her heart-shaped face.

"Isla, you look like a boss," Ricardo said with full approval before Evan could say anything. Then he cleared his throat, his cheeks flushing as he shot a glance at Evan, as if apologizing for being so informal.

Ricardo had always adored Isla, and before she'd started working here they'd been friendly. Or hell, friends. Isla had gotten Ricardo birthday presents and other little gifts throughout the year because, according to her, "He takes care of you, so I get to see you more."

She smiled, her own cheeks flushing pink. "Thanks. I figured this suit made a statement."

Ricardo nodded. "Definitely."

"Well, it's done," she said, turning to Evan, true joy in her voice. "Absolutely and completely done. We saved a lot of jobs and made a lot of money."

"Good. Hopefully you won't have to see that jackass anymore."

Ricardo let out a sort of strangled sound from the other side of the table and stared at his laptop as Isla's eyes widened. "Evan."

He shrugged. "I'm glad you wrapped up the deal. Look, about what you said last night."

Her gaze flicked over to Ricardo, then back at Evan, her eyebrows raised.

"About selling the company," he continued. His assistant was a vault, and would not repeat anything he said.

At his words, her shoulders relaxed as she stepped farther into the room and sat down at the conference table, stretching her lean legs out. "I just need all this behind me."

"I didn't realize you were going to actually sell it."

"I don't know what I'm going to do. I know I don't want the responsibility of all of this. It's not my dream, not even close to it. And if I had to work like this, live like this, it would kill me. But I also don't want a bunch of really incredible people screwed over either, so I'm still mulling over my options. If I sell, it's got to be to the right buyer."

"Sell it to me. Or we can just merge and I'll take over. I can make sure you're completely compensated and you can hold shares. You and your mother."

She blinked, straightening in her chair. "Seriously?"

"Why not? It's a good move."

She watched him for a long moment and he could practically see the wheels turning behind those beautiful green eyes. "Let's talk about it later."

"I'm not going to change my mind. No matter what happens between us," he murmured for her ears only. After last night they hadn't discussed their future or...anything. Though they had made love a few hours ago. He'd wanted to push her, to see where she stood on the subject of them, but he hadn't. Because he hadn't been sure he could deal with her answer if it wasn't what he wanted to hear.

Her cheeks tinged pink and she cleared her throat, glancing down the table at Ricardo, who was quietly talking into his Bluetooth. Evan knew the man well enough that he was definitely not paying attention to them right now. When he was focused on a task, nothing could distract him.

"Okay...I think we can figure something—" She turned at the sound of a knock on the door.

Evan glanced over as the door opened and Logan stepped in.

The head of security smiled warmly at Isla, then politely at him. "Some of the security team is throwing a going-away party for Ollie tonight. I know you're the boss, but I also know he would like it if you were there and he'd never ask himself. I can send you the details of the restaurant if you're interested," he said. "It'll be at seven o'clock. We've reserved a private room in the back, so it'll just be work people."

"I'll be there," she said.

"You're welcome too," Logan said to Evan.

Like there was any chance Evan was letting her go anywhere without him.

After the door had shut behind Logan, Isla turned to face Evan. "Don't even start," she said. "We're going. We'll make an appearance, I'll buy some drinks for everyone, and then we'll leave. He's been with the company a while and it wouldn't feel right to miss this."

"I didn't say anything."

"You didn't have to. You've got that look on your face."

"It's my resting bitchface," he said dryly.

She blinked before letting out a startled laugh. "I can't believe you just said that. I can't believe you actually know what that means."

His lips kicked up at the smile on her face. God, he loved seeing it. "I only know it because of Evie. She told me I have an RBF—and then explained to me what it was right before she punched me in the shoulder for some random offense."

Isla snickered. "I seriously love your sister."

Yeah, well, the feeling was mutual. His entire family loved Isla—even Ellis who was still on the run and in hiding—though not as much as Evan did. He just wanted her to be his again.

# CHAPTER TWENTY

"See? This place is totally secure." Isla nudged Evan gently in the side as they made their way through the dimly lit restaurant where people in business suits and skirts sat around tables, talking and drinking.

She'd already talked to Detective Duarte, and while he hadn't been thrilled that she was going out tonight, he'd assured her that Rodney was at his house under surveillance—and that they were about to make an arrest. Duarte was just getting his "ducks in a row" first.

She also knew that Evan had sent one of his own security guys from work over to the restaurant to do actual recon of this place before they arrived. She shouldn't be surprised but...she was touched. The last couple days with Evan—especially last night and this morning—had been sort of incredible. She was trying really hard not to think about their future or anything to do with them, relationship-wise. She was also failing, because it was pretty much all she could focus on. But it was too much pressure to worry about their future at the moment.

"I still don't have to like it." He kept his arm around her shoulders as they approached the hostess stand at the back room.

Isla loved the feel of him holding her close, even as it scared her that soon this would all be over. They'd go back to... She wasn't actually sure at this point. And she didn't want to think about it.

"Evan!" A female voice drew their attention to the left.

Isla kept her neutral smile in place as Rochelle Langer approached, wearing a skintight black dress and four-inch heels. And she wasn't wearing a bra either, Isla could clearly see. *Classy.*

The woman went in for air kisses, which Evan artfully dodged, and ended up giving her a weird, awkward hug.

Isla stifled a snort as Rochelle turned those green eyes on her, her expression calculating. Rochelle's mother had competed in pageants against Isla's mom, and Rochelle had always been weirdly competitive with her. The competition was one-sided though.

At that thought, she realized that her mother really was an artist for navigating the Miami social scene for so many decades. Isla simply couldn't do it. She'd never immersed herself in all the functions like her mother because she couldn't paste on a fake smile all the time and deal with the backstabbing.

"Isla, it's good to see you." Rochelle's gaze swept over her quickly, and clearly found her wanting.

Isla made a humming sound and smiled politely. That was all she could manage right now. She was still sore from falling down the stairs, emotionally dealing with being attacked, and even if she was with Evan right now, she was very aware that they weren't actually a couple.

"So is it true that you two are back together, or is that just gossip?" There was a definite glint in the woman's eyes as she teasingly skated her fingernails down Evan's forearm.

Isla blinked. Damn, she was bold tonight. And definitely drunk, if the glassy eyes were any indication.

"Yes, Isla took me back, thankfully." Evan kissed the top of Isla's head and pulled her even closer.

"Well, that's great," Rochelle said, though her body language screamed the exact opposite.

They made small talk for another sixty seconds—and yes, Isla was counting down in her head—before they were able to extricate themselves.

She was quiet as Evan spoke to the hostess and they made their way into the private room. All the faces were familiar, mostly men and women from the security division.

"What's wrong?" Evan asked quietly, keeping his arm snug around her.

Balloons had been strung up and a couple tables were decorated with signs wishing Ollie farewell. "What could be wrong?"

He squeezed her shoulder once, still not letting go of her as they headed up to one of the mini bars. "Come on."

"I don't want to talk about anything right now." Not here, surrounded by people she worked with—people who worked for her.

"Well too bad, we're going to talk about it." There was no give in his voice before he turned to the bartender and ordered two drinks for them.

She glanced around and saw that most people were in clusters talking and they wouldn't be overheard. "Fine. I just didn't like the way she was pawing at you, okay? It annoyed me. She annoyed me."

After taking the two glasses—champagne for her, she noticed in surprise, and a beer for him—he turned back to her.

"Champagne because you closed the deal today."

"Thank you," she murmured.

"Now," he said as they stepped away from the bar, "you can't seriously be bothered by Rochelle?"

She shrugged and took a sip. "I don't like her and I never have."

"Neither do I. Something you know. And you've never been jealous in the past."

"I've never been jealous, and I always thought it was because I was so evolved. But it turns out that I was never jealous because I never had a reason to be. Like I said last night, you and I," she said, lowering her voice even more, "we're not actually together. So that intangible thing that anchored me in our relationship before, that simple 'knowing' that you were mine and I was yours, well, it's gone. So I guess it just bothered me, seeing the way she was with you and knowing that as soon as this whole mess is over, and I go back to my normal life, you could start dating someone else. *Her*, for all I know."

The thought made her chest constrict. She was putting it all out there, building on some of her words last night and being honest and vulnerable. Though self-preservation told her to keep this stuff to herself, she simply couldn't play games. She had to be honest, to tell the truth. She wasn't going to tell him she was fine then stew all night.

He stared at her in surprise, his expression softening. "First of all, even if you and I had never met, I wouldn't be with that woman. Second, I don't want any other woman but you. After last night I thought that was clear. But obviously I need to be clearer. What I said about just being friends? I was lying to myself. I want you back more than anything, Isla. I'd sell my soul to turn back the clock. I know I don't deserve it and I understand if you can't give me a second chance. But I'm putting it all out there. I don't want a fake relationship. I want you and me for real. I'm sorry for what I did. More sorry than you can know. When I was lying in that hospital bed all I could think about was how you'd look at me with loathing over getting your father killed. I know that's not true now, but I was in a dark mental place and I'm still coming out of it. I've been trying to show you with action, not just words, that I'm here for good. But I will not walk away or push you away ever again. Not unless you tell me to go."

She stared up at him in shock, his words everything she'd wanted to hear. "What?"

"I'm sorry I'm dumping all this on you right now, but I don't ever want you to be jealous or feel insecure or even think about me with someone else. I just...I only want you. You're it for me. That's how I feel."

Her heart pounded a staccato rhythm. "I don't know what to say." He'd pretty much just laid out everything she'd needed to hear from him.

"Don't say anything. Just think about what I said. I know I can't expect things to go back to where they were, but I'd like to start fresh with you."

She stared at him, trying to find the right words—something, anything—but they were interrupted.

"Thank you guys for coming tonight," Ollie said as he approached her and Evan, a big smile on his face.

She forced a smile of her own, wishing he hadn't just interrupted the most important moment of her life. "Of course. We're going to miss you."

"Thanks. Listen, if you have a second, can I talk to you in private?"

Evan's grip around her shoulders tightened ever so slightly, but she subtly nudged him. "Of course. I see a free corner over there." She'd already given him a great reference and he'd been hired on to a new company, so she wondered what this could be about. And the sooner they were done, the sooner she could get back to Evan and finish their discussion.

Aware of Evan's eyes on her back as she headed over to a semi-quiet corner with Ollie, she tuned him out as much as she could. Which wasn't easy to do after what he'd just said. Could she and Evan really start over and make a new life together? She was afraid to even hope for that.

"So what's up?"

"Look, I know it's not my last day, but I'm only going to be here for the rest of the week and... It's probably nothing, but I think Logan might have a gambling problem. I don't know if it's serious or what, but I've noticed a few things on his computer, and I've seen him gambling online—not during work hours or anything, but in our line of work I know that can leave us susceptible to certain things. Especially with how much access we have to security. I feel weird telling you since he's my superior, but..." He lifted his shoulders.

"Thank you for telling me." Because he was right. Any sort of addiction left anyone open to blackmail or exploitation, and considering the kind of access Logan had, that wasn't a good thing. "This stays between us."

The tension in his shoulders eased. "Good. And sorry to bring up work here, I just needed to get it off my chest. And now I'm going to get back to the party. I hope you guys can stay for a while."

She simply smiled as he headed back to talk to some of his security buddies, and before she'd taken two steps Evan was at her side. "Is everything okay?"

"Yeah. I'm ready to get out of here though. Let's say a quick hello to a few more people and then sneak out?" She'd talked to the guy the party was being thrown for, so she'd done her duty. She and Evan had important, unfinished business that needed her immediate attention. Though...she wasn't sure what she was going to say to him, how to respond.

"Sounds good to me. And look, I paid off the first tab. So if they run up anything after we leave, it's on whoever else is here."

She looked up at him in surprise. "You're very sneaky."

"I gave one of the servers my card when you were talking to Ollie, and he already ran it."

"That's very sweet, Evan. Especially since none of these people work with you."

He grinned at her. "If you sell me the company, maybe that will change."

He'd definitely given her something to think about with his offer. But she had other things on her mind now.

After talking to a couple more people, they discreetly left.

Once they were in the warmth of Evan's luxury vehicle, she settled against the leather seat, suddenly nervous about being alone after everything he'd admitted. She wasn't ready to give him an answer yet, and scrambled for something else to say. "Ollie said he thinks Logan might have a gambling problem," she said into the quiet.

Evan glanced at her in surprise. "Seriously?"

"Yep. I have a feeling the only reason he's telling me is because he's leaving, so it doesn't feel disloyal. Lizzy already got back to me and said she could start working on our system Friday." Lizzy with Red Stone had incredible qualifications, and Isla was having outside people do an audit no matter what. "I want to ask her to look into all of our employees, but especially anyone in security."

"Good."

"It just feels weird to me. Invasive." And she didn't like this aspect of her job.

"It's part of running a company this size. You've got to keep things secure. For everyone's sake."

Yeah, well, she'd feel better once she was no longer running the company, once all the responsibility was out of her hands. This kind of job, of life, was perfect for some people. But not for her.

She didn't even want to think about anything work related now, not when she kept turning over Evan's words in her mind. He'd told her everything she'd wanted to hear from him, and now? She was scared to trust him again.

# CHAPTER TWENTY-ONE

As he approached the back of the one-story ranch-style house, he tugged his gloves on. There'd been a police car doing surveillance across the street earlier, but they'd been called away for something—he'd hacked into their scanners. He'd planned to call in a distraction himself, but a real call was even better for his purposes. Nothing could get traced back to him.

Now everything was ready. He had a problem he needed to take care of and he couldn't wait any longer. Once he eliminated this threat, he had to toss down a few breadcrumb trails before he made his move to take what he wanted. What he deserved.

Isla.

Careful to stick to the shadows of the yard, he quickly disabled the security lights on the back porch with an expertly thrown rock taken from the yard. Picking the lock was a little more difficult and took more time than he would like, but he'd been practicing. His target didn't have a security system, but if the man had, he'd have taken care of that as well.

He was quiet as he stepped into the kitchen, listening for movement. Moonlight streamed in from the small window above a sink filled to the brim with dishes. There were enough outside lights and nightlights that he had a perfect visual of the interior.

He'd never been inside the house before but he had the layout memorized thanks to architectural plans he'd stolen. There were two bedrooms on the right side of the house, and he was fairly certain the bigger one was the master. It only made sense. So he knew which way he was going.

At three in the morning, there was no movement or noise. No television going, no one working on their computer, nothing.

His rubber-soled shoes were silent as he quietly stepped from the kitchen into a hallway. Another nightlight was plugged into the wall, giving him a little illumination, but most of the house was dark.

His heart raced as he peered around the end of the hallway. Empty. And still quiet.

His prey would be sleeping.

As he hurried down the next hallway, his heart rate kicked into high gear. He'd killed before, but only ever women. And he hadn't tried to disguise the kills as suicide. Tonight would be different, so he had to be smart about this.

It had to look good. This whole scene had to be convincing.

He glanced into what he assumed was a guest room and found out it was an office—empty.

Next he eased open the already cracked bedroom door and found who he was looking for.

His target was sleeping, turned on his side, looking peaceful as anything. This man needed to die for multiple reasons. He'd hurt Isla, who didn't belong to him. And he needed to be gone so she felt safe again. So she wouldn't have a protector 24/7. He needed Bishop out of the way so he could get to Isla. And this was the best way to do it.

Adrenaline surging, he reached into his back pocket to pull out the chloroform and cloth. It was quick-dissolving and nearly impossible to detect in an autopsy.

As he approached the bed, blood rushed in his ears, power flooding through his body as he leaned down close.

As if the man sensed something, a shift in the air maybe, his victim's eyes popped open in confusion. Before he could really appreciate the visible fear, he shoved the cloth over the man's face.

The man's arms flailed out but stilled almost immediately, his entire body going lax.

He smiled as he stepped back, his dick rock-hard as he thought of what was to come. Killing always did this to him. Always got him hard. He'd have to jerk off later, but for now there was nothing to do about it.

Now it was time to get to work. He had to set the stage and make sure everything was perfect for when the cops found the body.

\* \* \*

Hours later as he rode up the elevator of the high-rise where he had access to an empty, bank-owned condo, he smiled about what he'd done.

The cops were too stupid to figure out anything. He was too smart for all of them. He'd killed others before tonight and never been caught. It was always people who got in his way. Some hands-on, others hands-off, as in the case of the bombing at Bishop's company. But it was always the same outcome. Get in the way of his wants or desires? Then you died.

He wished he had someone to share his handiwork with, to show off to.

He wanted to tell Isla. But he couldn't tell her anything. She would never understand. He'd thought she'd liked him, that she could be with him. But she was back with Bishop.

Some of his good mood started to fade as he reached the top floor. He shouldn't be here but he'd hacked into the security and wiped a record of his presence. No one would know.

Besides, he simply had to see her. Had to know what she was doing. It was a long shot, but he would try.

In the empty penthouse of the foreclosed condo, his shoes were barely perceptible against the tile as he made his way to where the tripod and long-range camera were set up.

This was the kind of stuff the paparazzi used and it was worth every penny.

As he dropped his duffel bag on the ground next to the equipment, he stepped up to the camera and looked

BISHOP'S QUEEN | 193

through the lens. It took a moment to adjust, but it was pointed where it always was.

Evan Bishop's condo. The windows had automatic blinds, but the man didn't always keep them shut. Why would he, when he was so high up with no one to look in?

Isla used to stay there at Bishop's high-rise all the time and he'd watched her. Watched her and Bishop together.

He'd tried to get a visual of her place but hadn't been able to because of the way the building was angled. Hadn't mattered anyway because she'd always been at Bishop's. He snarled in disgust.

Thankfully he was able to see right into the master bedroom.

He nearly jerked back when he saw Isla staring right out the window, completely naked except for some kind of filmy robe. It was as if she was looking right at him.

Just like that his dick got hard again.

She was beautiful, her long hair flowing around her shoulders and breasts as she took a sip of something from a mug. Probably tea.

He snapped a picture.

He started to pull his dick out of his pants, then Bishop appeared out of nowhere, moving in behind her and wrapping a blanket and then his arms around her. He leaned down and nuzzled Isla's neck, probably whispered something dirty to her.

Anger punched through him. That should be *him*. Should be *him* holding her. Turning her on. But the whore had made her decision.

Gripping himself, he stroked in hard, angry pulls. She was his, no one else's. Not Bishop's. Only *his*.

And if he couldn't have her, no one could.

Before he killed her, he was going to get a taste of what he'd been missing.

Maybe when he finally killed her, he'd be able to move on, get over this terrible obsession with her.

# CHAPTER TWENTY-TWO

Isla looked up and found Evan watching her across the conference room table. For some ridiculous reason she found her cheeks warming under that intense gaze. "What?" she asked.

"Just thinking about how beautiful you are."

She blinked, her cheeks going even warmer. "If I didn't know you, I'd say that sounds like a line."

"No line, just the truth. And I'm not talking about looks either, though you are beautiful. I just... Waking up to you the last couple mornings has meant a lot to me. *You* mean a lot to me."

She leaned back in her chair, watching him carefully, surprised at how honest he was being, how vulnerable he was letting himself be right now. A tiny kernel of hope popped inside her. He'd told her he wanted to show her with action, not just words, how much she meant to him. Well, the words mattered too, and she hadn't realized how much she needed them. He'd never been super vocal—except in the bedroom. This "extra" from him was different, but she liked it.

"Last night was very nice," she murmured, thinking about what they'd done once they'd gotten to his place after the going-away party. She hadn't been ready to give him an answer about "them" and thankfully he hadn't pushed. But he had gotten her naked. So, very naked.

196 | KATIE REUS

Aaaand she really cursed her redheaded coloring right now because there was no hiding the growing blush across her cheeks.

Evan let out a low growl as his gaze dipped to her mouth. He'd started to respond when the conference room door opened.

Carol stepped in, efficient as always. "I'm sorry to interrupt you, but there's a Detective Duarte here to see you. I knew you'd want to see him right away. I think he has news." She whispered the last part and ducked out.

As her nerves started to prickle at the thought of possible news, Isla shut her laptop and Evan did the same. Then she gathered the few papers and placed them facedown on the conference table as the detective was shown into the room. It wasn't that she didn't trust him not to see what they were working on, but they had a lot of privacy clauses with most of their contracts that they had to be conscious of.

"Detective," she said, standing and motioning for him to sit.

"I'm good, but thanks. This shouldn't take too long."

"Would you like anything to drink or eat?" Carol asked, standing in the open doorway. Her dark hair was pulled back into a chic twist at her neck and her dark blue wrap dress matched her eyes.

He shook his head and Isla's assistant quickly ducked out, the door shutting with a soft whoosh behind her.

"Good news?" Isla asked. She knew he was supposed to have gotten the warrant this morning for Rodney's house and computer, and she'd already turned over everything she could from his work computer. And, well, the detective had to be here for a reason. The man was far too busy to simply stop by to talk.

"I have news. Rodney Wood is dead." His tone was neutral, his gaze just as flat as he delivered the information.

She blinked then glanced at Evan in surprise—and by the brief flicker in his gaze, he was surprised too. They both looked back at the detective.

"What happened?" Evan asked before she could.

Despite what he said before, the detective took a seat at the end of the table, facing both of them. "Looks like a suicide. I shouldn't give you all the details but I'm going to use some discretion. He overdosed and...he had a sort of shrine to you," he said, focusing on her. "It looks as if he's been stalking you for a little while."

*Uh, say what?* "Seriously? He didn't even seem to like me."

The detective lifted a shoulder. "There's a lot of evidence that says he was behind poisoning you and the attack at the hospital. He's had issues with women before—domestic ones."

"What?" She couldn't believe she didn't know about this. Her company had strict policies in place regarding things like domestic violence.

"Nothing on record because the charges were always dropped. Anyway, he left a note—a confession of sorts. I have no idea if the note is real as it hasn't been analyzed, but the scene itself...it looks real. He had a few security badges that were definitely not his own, giving him access to this building, and his prints were all over them. And he had a uniform of one of the food delivery services you use. It would explain how he got into your office undetected. We're going to review the feeds and see what we can find, but since we already know he hacked the security system, I'm not sure what we'll find if he's erased the original feeds."

"You're sure he's the one who hacked the system?" Isla asked.

"A cursory look at his computer says yes. Our tech people are going to dig deeper but it looks as if he's guilty. I'm not sure on everything yet, but I will cross all T's and dot all I's."

She allowed relief to slide through her at the detective's words. Still... "It's just weird. I never got the feeling that he was into me. You said he had a shrine to me? What exactly does that mean?"

Clearing his throat, he shifted uncomfortably. "He had pictures of you. Taken from a long-range camera. You are not completely dressed in all of them."

She felt sick to her stomach as his words settled in. "Oh my God, like naked pictures? He was watching me?" She wrapped her arms around herself and before she could blink Evan had rounded the table and sat right next to her, his big body vibrating with rage.

"Nobody better see any pictures of Isla," he snapped to the detective. "Those aren't going to get entered into any sort of evidence where people could take them. If they do, I'll sue your entire department."

BISHOP'S QUEEN | 199

Duarte sighed. "Look, I've already set the pictures aside and I'm going to be removing them from the file. This was a suicide—or it appears to be—and there's no need for us to keep these pictures. I guarantee your privacy will be kept." He looked between the both of them, his expression sincere.

Some tension eased inside her, but it grossed her out to know that Rodney had pictures of her—had been watching her. Even though he was dead, icy shivers still streaked down her spine. "Did your guys find him when...when you went to deliver the warrant?"

He nodded and stood, looking down at his phone which was buzzing insistently.

"You're really sure it's suicide?"

"It looks that way, but we're still doing an autopsy. The pills are in his name, the scene looks right to me, but...I'm going to make sure everything is in order. I want to make sure you can close this chapter for good. I want to make sure you're safe."

There was so much damn sincerity in his expression and voice and she understood what made him such a good detective. The man truly cared. "Thank you for letting me know," she said. "I know you didn't have to come down here personally and I really appreciate it. I'm still having someone run an audit on our security system. They're supposed to come in tomorrow."

"Lizzy from Red Stone, right?" He pulled his buzzing phone out again, frowned at the screen.

She blinked. "How do you know that?"

"Ah, she's my former partner's sister-in-law. I've really got to take this. Call me if you need anything." He didn't wait for her response, just hurried from the room as he answered the call.

Isla turned in her seat and let Evan take her hands in his.

"It's over," he murmured, kissing her knuckles.

She closed her eyes for a moment. "I'm glad the threat is over, but it still feels weird that he's dead." She didn't feel guilty because it wasn't her fault, but it was still an odd feeling knowing that he had killed himself, that he'd been stalking her, had tried to kill her. Twice. And now he was just...gone.

Evan leaned forward and brushed his lips over hers, a soothing kiss, nothing more. And it was exactly what she needed.

Sighing, she laid her forehead against his for a long moment. Then she leaned back but didn't let go of his hands. His touch was grounding in the most familiar way. "Thank you for being here through everything."

"I'm not going anywhere," he said quietly. "I know you don't want any more apologies, but if you let me, I want to continue being there for you. I'm not giving up on us."

"I think we need to take things one day at a time. Maybe go on a date?" They'd jumped into sex and her staying at his place so quickly. The staying over had to do with security reasons, but the sex? It was fantastic, yet she wasn't sure it was the smartest choice.

She so desperately wanted to believe that he was sincere, that he wouldn't bolt at the first sign of difficulty. And she believed that *he* believed his own words. His sincerity was true. But deep down, she was scared of getting hurt again. She'd trusted him more than she'd ever trusted anyone, and at the first sign of real trouble, he'd cut her out of his life.

"How about I take you out tomorrow night? There's a movie showing down at the wharf."

If he knew that, he must have been thinking ahead. The thought made her smile. "I think that sounds like a plan. And don't expect to get lucky after."

"I would never expect—but I will be hopeful." His lips kicked up slightly, that charming, sexy man she knew right at the forefront. "And since I know your favorite things, I'll pack a picnic basket."

Her heart melted just a little bit at his words. This felt normal, right, and even though she was afraid to jump straight into things again, she was still going to give him a chance. He'd hurt her before, had stomped all over her heart, but... She believed that he was sorry. And she believed in second chances. She wasn't naïve enough to think everyone deserved one. But he did. And living without him was worse than the fear of getting hurt again.

"I'll need to move some things from your place back to mine." She'd brought far too many things over, including most of her toiletries.

He stilled at her words. "Yeah, I guess you will. Unless..."

"Unless what?"

"Unless you just want to stay."

Oh, how she wanted to. Desperately, in fact. She wanted to tell him yes, but if they were going to start fresh, she wanted to truly start fresh. And that meant getting to know each other again. Even if the sex was toe-curling, sheet-scorching hot. Once he was able to take his shirt off in front of her, to truly be okay with his scars, she knew they'd be ready to move forward. That wasn't something she could push either. He simply had to trust in them.

"Not tonight. But we'll see how tomorrow goes." And she didn't have to be a fortune-teller to know that she would very likely end up in his bed. Under him and on top of him. But after today she could admit she needed some downtime, to decompress and wrap her head around everything that had gone down. That the man who'd tried to kill her was gone, no longer a threat.

There was a knock on the door again, and when she glanced over she saw Carol standing there, her expression apologetic. "You've got two waiting calls. One from Mr. Conti and the other from Ms. Caldwell with Red Stone. I put them both on hold because I wasn't sure who was priority."

"Give me a second. I'll take Lizzy's call in my office. Ask Geno if I can call him back?"

Carol nodded as Isla stood and turned to Evan. "I've got to take these calls. And with Rodney... Well, with him not a problem anymore, you don't have to stay here at the office anymore. I know it's been a pain for you to work here."

Evan shrugged. "It hasn't been a pain. I'll work here the rest of the day. I like being close to you," he said bluntly.

"I like it too." Way too much. God, maybe she was a fool, but she was going to risk her heart again. She loved the man too much not to.

A few moments later she was in her office. "Hey, Lizzy. Everything okay?"

"Everything's great. My current job ended quicker than I thought. I wanted to see if you want me to come by this afternoon and start my audit early?" she asked.

"Yes, that's fantastic. Look," Isla said, "I talked to Detective Duarte today and he said that he knew you were running an audit on our security system." And she was slightly annoyed that Lizzy had told the other man. Stuff like this was supposed to be confidential. She hadn't even told her own security team.

"Yes, and I'm really sorry he even knows that. He and his wife were over at my brother-in-law Grant's place last night along with a bunch of family. He asked me to do him a favor and contact you about looking into your security. He said his guys were working on the case and he wanted me to act as a consultant of sorts. So I told him I'd already been hired. The second the words were out I knew I shouldn't have said anything, but—"

"No, that's totally fine. That's actually understandable. He got a call and I didn't get to push him more on how he knew." She went on to tell Lizzy about what she'd

204 | KATIE REUS

learned this morning about the man stalking her. "I know he's dead, but I still want to look at anything related to him as well. And all of my security people. When do you think you'll be here?"

"In about two hours."

"Sounds good."

Next she called Geno, and was surprised when he wanted to set up a dinner with her. Not a date, but simply dinner because he wanted to talk to her about something. Though she was sick to death of business dinners, she couldn't say no to the man. Despite what Evan thought about him, she genuinely liked Geno. And she thought that if he ever stepped out of his father's and brother's shadows, he would find his footing in the world.

As she wrapped up the call, she looked up to Evan stepping into her office, carrying a mug with little white wisps of steam rolling off the top.

"Your favorite," he murmured, setting it on the desk.

Once again she was struck by how normal this felt, how very "them" this was. She'd missed him so much. "Thank you... I've missed you, Evan. I've missed us."

His eyes flared slightly, heat simmering in them. "I've missed us too." Then he cleared his throat. "Everything good with Lizzy?"

"Yes. She's actually going to start her audit early so I'm going to let the security crew know that she'll be given full access to everything when she gets here."

"You're telling them now?"

She shook her head as she picked up the drink. "I'm going to spring this on them."

"Good idea. Look, I know we're going out tomorrow, but can I take you out to dinner tonight?"

She winced slightly. "I can't. I want to say yes, but Geno wanted to meet up about something."

"A date?" His tone was dry.

She snorted softly. "No. He said he wanted to run something by me."

His body language was tense. "All right then, tomorrow it is."

She narrowed her eyes at him. "You're being awfully calm about this."

"I might not like the guy, but it's only because I'm a jealous asshole. I know there's nothing going on between the two of you."

"That's a good answer. And you're not an asshole."

He lifted a shoulder. "According to some people I am."

"Not according to me." Not too long ago she'd have lumped him into the asshole category easily. But now?

Now was all about second chances.

# CHAPTER TWENTY-THREE

"Thanks for meeting me here." Geno stood as Isla reached the little round table outside the hole-in-the-wall tapas place.

"No problem. I've heard this place is incredible." She shed her coat and sat across from him.

"It is. I've only been here once, but I plan to change that."

The exterior patio had a dozen small mosaic-tile-covered tables. Since it was chilly out, heating lamps had been placed strategically throughout the outdoor seating. Instrumental guitar music played softly from the speakers and before she'd settled in a server appeared, taking her drink order and an order of empanadas for the table.

"So what's up?" She settled back in the small metal chair, glad it had a cushion on the seat. "You said you had something to talk to me about."

"Yeah. I know our project is over. What you said about selling your father's company, about doing what you want, kinda hit me in a good way. I'm thinking of leaving my family's company and breaking out on my own."

Her eyebrows lifted in surprise.

"I'm not sure if your surprise is a good reaction or not," he said lightly as the server dropped their drinks off and promised their empanadas would be out shortly.

"It's just a reaction, not good or bad, I promise. So...why are you telling me this?"

He lifted a shoulder and gone was the smooth, charming Geno with the quick smile. "Truthfully, because I respect your opinion. You're selling your dad's company and going out on your own to do...whatever it is you're planning. That's huge. We've worked together and I've seen how driven and smart you are. I wanted to get your opinion."

"Oh," she said, surprised.

"I have no one else to talk to about this. Lately I've realized that I have lived a very shallow life, and that kind of self-evaluation is not pretty." There was more than a touch of self-loathing in his voice.

*All right, then.* "So what are you planning on doing?"

"That's the problem. I don't know. I know I'm good with money and I'm good with numbers. I also know that I have a reputation—an earned one—but I got into college with my grades. And I didn't skate by, for the record. I graduated with honors, to the surprise of my family." He shrugged. "Math makes sense to me and I like it when numbers make sense. I like...fixing things. What I don't like is working crazy hours, wearing suits, and not feeling like I'm making a difference."

"I actually understand that."

"So what are you doing when you leave?" he asked.

"To start, I'm expanding a current community center and I'm planning on building a new one on the west side of town. The state and federal funding is complete crap and there aren't nearly enough local services, especially for a city this size. I'd already started planning everything before my dad..." She cleared her throat. "Anyway, I think we can do a lot of good and create some fantastic after-school programs. I've got a lot of experience in dealing with commercial construction. I've got more plans after, but for now, this will be my immediate focus."

"That's right," he murmured. "You were a project manager in that division before the bombing..." Now he was the one who cleared his throat. "Well, that's really cool."

"Thanks. I kinda think so." She was ready to put her business and construction management degrees to use, ready to really jump into projects she was passionate about. And this was where she wanted to start.

They talked all throughout dinner and she was glad that she hadn't judged him too harshly. There was a lot more to Geno than most people realized.

"I'm still not sure what I want to do," he said as he picked up the bill from the table. "But I feel more focused now. Maybe you should think about consulting or therapy for shallow partiers."

She laughed at his assessment and pulled out a couple twenties, tossing them onto the table to leave a nice tip. "That's one thing to consider."

For the first time in ages, she felt as if a weight had been lifted. Her father was gone and the hurt from that would never go away. But she could finally see an end in sight to all the work she'd been doing.

And Evan was back in her life. That, more than anything, changed her entire world again. In a good way. It terrified her, but she wanted to take a chance on them.

# CHAPTER TWENTY-FOUR

Even though Evan was agitated that Isla was out with Conti tonight, he wasn't going to be an asshole about it. With Rodney dead and Lizzy running full diagnostics on Isla's company, he felt nominally better. Still, when Nic Bentley sent him some video feeds from the party, he'd jumped on them.

The asshole had felt bad—or said he did—about Isla getting hurt on his property. Evan was pretty sure Bentley was just worried about her suing him, so he was bending over backward to be accommodating. At least this gave Evan something to do tonight instead of obsessing about her out with Conti.

After the last couple days he felt like they were headed in the right direction but he had a long way to go in making things right with Isla. And it was going to be one step at a time, he'd realized. There wasn't a magic wand he could wave to make things better. He was still going to have to eventually be comfortable enough to reveal his scars. Otherwise, they'd never be able to move on.

Leaning forward in his desk chair, he sped up the feeds, glancing over a lot of familiar faces. Frowning as he got a flash of someone surprising, he rewound then paused when he saw a familiar face on-screen.

A face he was surprised to see at Nic Bentley's party. Grabbing his cell phone, he dialed Bentley, already cursing the guy out. If he didn't answer—

To his surprise the man answered on the second ring and sounded sober. "Hey Bishop, what's up?"

"I'm looking at the security feed you sent me."

"Yeah, look, really sorry about your lady. I wish I'd gotten a chance to talk to her at the party."

"You had a chance but you blew us off multiple times."

There was a pause. "Yeah, I'm sorry about that. I'd been drinking a lot. Anyway, I hope you can use the security feeds for something. And if she's going to sue me, hopefully she gives me a heads-up."

Evan tempered his annoyance and decided not to even comment. "Listen, I see someone on-screen I'm surprised was at the party. Oliver Mulaney. Did you invite him?"

"Oh yeah, that guy is all right. I've used him to hack—" He cleared his throat. "Ah, I use him to do some off-the-books work for me. A friend of mine recommended him. He's wicked good with computers."

Ice slid through Evan's veins. "Did you know he works for Isla's company?"

"Yeah, he mentioned it. In security or something. But he's leaving for another job or something. Look, I'm not using him for anything pertaining to her!" Panic coated his words as he seemed to understand where Evan was going with this, and he could practically see the guy sweating out the whiskey he seemed to favor. "Or you, for that matter. I got into some trouble and I needed him to erase—"

"I don't give a fuck. Who recommended him to you?" After Bentley told him what he needed to know, Evan hung up. This didn't feel right. He pressed play and watched as Ollie looked over at someone in the crowd. Zooming in on the man as much as he could, and keeping the sound muted so he didn't have to hear the party going on, he looked hard at him.

Ollie's eyes narrowed and he blew off a woman trying to talk to him as he watched something. Someone. Evan zoomed out and realized Ollie had spotted him and Isla arriving. A man walked across the screen, blocking Ollie for a moment, but then the view was clear again. He was still watching Isla, his anger clear even in the video. Not just anger—rage.

Alarm bells were going off in Evan's head and he wasn't going to ignore them. Maybe this was nothing. But it might be something.

Grabbing his keys and cell phone, he hurried out of the condo and called Isla. She didn't answer so he texted her what he'd found. Once in the elevator he called Lizzy, unsure if she was still working.

She answered on the first ring. "Hey, is Isla with you?" she asked, not bothering with small talk.

"No, but I'm going to find her right now." He needed to have eyes on her. To know she was safe. Everything about this felt wrong. And Ollie had unlimited access to the security at the building— *Hell.* He could have easily hacked the system. What if he had something to do with the hacking or stalking?

"Good. Something weird is going on with her security system. Most of the guys were all right with me looking at their feeds and system, but I could tell my audit bothered a few people. Anyway, I looked at the spreadsheets of the issues they've been having, and like Ollie Mulaney told you guys, there was definitely a glitch in the system. But it was completely avoidable. Those updates would've happened automatically. That glitch was intentional. Someone set this up to create a backdoor into the system. I'm not going to explain why because it doesn't matter, but that's what happened. And looking deeper, someone has been spying on Isla. Not work stuff, but using her laptop camera to spy on her."

"Who?" he demanded as he reached the bottom floor, his heart racing.

"I don't know yet. I found some traces of files that someone tried to erase. And they did a really good job. Professional. But nothing is ever truly gone."

"Look at Ollie. I think he's stalking her." Evan wasn't going on much at this point other than the video he'd just seen and his gut. He jumped into his SUV and tore out of the parking lot.

"I've already started digging into him. It was clear my presence here today bothered him, so I started with his files. I've also found out some other interesting things but I'll tell Isla when I talk to her."

BISHOP'S QUEEN | 215

"So I have a huge favor to ask. Can you find out where she is right now?" He gave her the name of a local restaurant Isla had told him she was meeting Geno at. He hoped she was still there.

"Hold on. She gave me full access to her electronics, so just give me a sec. Okay she's at the restaurant and..." He heard soft clicking in the background, then Lizzy swore. "Someone else is monitoring her phone."

"What?"

"Yes. There's spyware on it and I can see that someone is actually monitoring her in real time."

"I'll call you back." He hung up and dialed Isla. She didn't answer so he called two more times, then texted again. *Damn it.* He never should have let her out of his sight.

When he approached a red light, but didn't see cars coming on either side, he floored it. If a cop tried to pull him over, well, good luck. He wasn't stopping for anything.

As he made another sharp turn, a horn blasted but he ignored it as he gunned the engine. When Isla didn't answer again, he gritted his teeth and called Geno.

"Hello?" Geno said, the sound of guitar music playing in the background.

"Conti, it's Bishop. Is Isla with you?"

"Jesus Christ, there's nothing going on between us," Conti snapped. "I just wanted to talk to her about—"

"I don't care. I think she's in danger. Where is she?"

According to Lizzy she was still at the restaurant and he

just hoped Conti was too. "I need you to get eyes on her now."

"Shit. She just left. Hold on, she's walking across the street now. She got curbside parking. Let me try to flag her down." There was a rustling in the background as if Geno was running.

*Come on, come on,* Evan silently shouted.

"Damn it, she didn't see me."

Evan knew she'd probably turned off her ringer during dinner because that was just the way she was, but damn it. "All right, thanks—"

"Oh my God!" Geno shouted into the phone.

"What?" He took another turn, gunning the engine. He was barely five minutes out. He willed time to speed up for him, to get there faster.

"A truck just smashed into the front of her car. Oh, God." Evan could hear the sound of him running now. "He's taking her! Ollie is kidnapping Isla!"

Panic punched through Evan. He started to hang up to call an ambulance, but froze when he heard Geno's voice, laced with terror. "Put the gun down."

*Pop. Pop.*

"Geno!" he shouted, but the line went dead.

# CHAPTER TWENTY-FIVE

E van took one last sharp turn as he called Lizzy. She picked up immediately. "I think Ollie just shot Geno and kidnapped Isla." He felt as if he'd floated out of his body, as if this couldn't be happening.

"Shit. Where?" Her tone was matter-of-fact and it somehow grounded him.

He had to be calm for Isla. Because he was getting her back. "At the tapas place. I was talking to Geno when someone slammed into Isla's car. He said Ollie was taking Isla and then I'm pretty sure he was shot." He really hoped the other man was okay.

"Her phone is showing that it's still near the restaurant so it didn't go with her. I'm hacking into the DMV cameras now. Do you know what he was driving?"

"No. But—"

"Don't worry about it. I've got the video of the crash now." He could hear typing softly in the background. "He's in a truck and I've got the license plate."

"He's going to take her somewhere. Somewhere he owns. Look up his address or any properties he owns. He won't want to go far and he'll want to stash his truck."

"Hush. Let me work. And I've already done that."

Time seemed to stretch as he made a right, driving by Isla's smashed-in car. He saw a crowd gathered around someone. Had to be Geno. He wanted to stop, but someone would've called the cops by now. And he couldn't do anything for Geno. But he could save Isla. If they could just figure out where she was being held or where Ollie was driving.

He'd do anything to find her. Including sell his soul.

"Got it! It's an older truck and it's headed down Lockwood Street. He has a push bar on it. It's how he got away without damage."

His heart rate kicked up. "He's driving that way in real time?" he asked as he pressed on the gas, heading in that direction.

"Yes. Give me a second..." More typing. "He's headed toward a residential area. Older neighborhoods. And... He owns a couple properties. Including one left to him by his grandmother. She's dead but she left him the truck and the house. He's tried to hide that he still owns the house. He put it up for sale, then a trust bought it and I'm ninety-nine percent sure he owns that trust." Suddenly she let out a curse.

"What?" His phone pinged and a message popped up from Lizzy with an address. Before he could ask what it was, she continued.

"I can't track the vehicle anymore. It's an '88 Ford. Black. He's got newer vehicles than the one he's driving tonight. I can't tell you with one hundred percent accuracy that this is where he's headed, but he went to some trouble to hide that he owns this place. I've texted you the address."

"Thank you. I owe you everything."

He hung up and called Detective Duarte as he took a hard turn, ignoring the horns honking in his wake. Everything around him funneled out as he drove, his one mission to save Isla.

"Oliver Mulaney kidnapped Isla. I think he's been stalking her. And I think I know where he's taking her. He shot Geno Conti." His movements jerky as he took another turn. According to his GPS he was minutes out from the house. But it wasn't fast enough.

"What the hell?" the detective shouted.

"I don't have time to explain any of it. He owns a couple properties and I think he's taking her to one of them."

"Give me the address." He did and then Duarte said, "I'm on my way and sending a team over. Do not go in without—"

Evan hung up. The detective called him back but he silenced his phone.

He'd been a Marine—and once a Marine, always one. And even if he hadn't been, no one was keeping him from Isla. He would die to save her. But he wanted to live. They deserved a shot at a future.

*Hold on*, he mentally shouted, praying with all that he had that she was still alive.

## CHAPTER TWENTY-SIX

Isla opened her eyes, blinking against the lights as pain filtered through her head… She didn't recognize these lights or the popcorn ceiling. She didn't even know houses had those anymore—

Panic punched through her as everything came rushing back.

Someone had plowed into her car and then Ollie had been there. She'd been confused to see him, then… Maybe he'd put something over her face. Then she remembered nothing. Groaning, she tried to sit up and realized her wrists and ankles were tied.

*Oh no.*

"You're awake," a familiar voice said as Ollie stepped out of the shadows of the bathroom.

Fear curdled inside her, making bile rise up. She twisted her neck as he approached. "What are you doing?" Even as she asked, she knew it was a stupid question because he'd obviously kidnapped her—after smashing into her car.

He sat on the edge of the bed and ran his finger down her forearm.

She tried to pull away, instinctively not wanting his touch.

That rejection brought her a slap across the cheek.

Face stinging, ears ringing, she closed her eyes as she tried to think. If she wanted to get out of this alive, she had to be smart.

"You think you're too good for me?" he growled, his voice right next to her ear.

She didn't open her eyes, didn't want to see him. Didn't want this to be real. Ohgodohgodohgod how was this happening? Why was this happening?

"If Bishop had just died, none of this would have happened." His voice was farther away now.

She hadn't even realized he'd gotten off the bed, hadn't felt him move. Blood was rushing in her ears so loudly that it was all she could do to think above the screaming in her own head. She opened her eyes to find him standing at the foot of the bed, watching her. Subtly she tried to tug on the bindings but they dug into her wrists, chafing.

"What do you mean?" she asked carefully, keeping her voice as neutral and calm as possible, though she wobbled on the last word.

"In the bombing. He should have died."

*Wait...what?* She felt all the blood leave her face. "You were behind the bombing?" Again she tried to keep her voice calm, but her father had died in that explosion. Evan had almost died. She'd lost so much. A lot of people had.

His smile went full-on evil Cheshire cat. "I black-mailed John Nix into doing it. It was either that or let his enemies know about the existence of his little girl. The guy's a psycho but he would do anything for her. All I had to do was show him a few pictures of her leaving school and threaten to let some very bad people know and he did whatever I wanted." And Ollie sounded completely smug about it.

He was calling someone else a psycho? "You killed my dad?" She stared at him in horror, unable to hide her disgust.

"I didn't want to!" he shouted, his face going red with rage. "What choice did I have! He was getting close to firing me."

She frowned, not understanding. Her father hadn't told her everything, but he'd never mentioned firing Ollie.

"Oh yes, he was keeping it very close to the vest. I diverted a few funds from some stagnant accounts and he caught on. He didn't know I was behind it, but he was getting close to figuring things out. He had to go."

"But...everyone else," she whispered, tugging on the ropes.

"Once I had the idea to kill him, it was easy to add Bishop to the list and it just made sense. I don't understand what you ever saw in him!" He wasn't smiling anymore.

And Isla knew better than to say anything about Evan or why she was with him. Nothing she said would help.

"I didn't want to kill the others, but they were collateral damage." He started pacing at the end of the bed, his movements jerky.

"Why did you poison me?" That was one thing she didn't understand. Not that she understood him regardless, but she didn't understand the motive in trying to kill her, then bringing her here. He could have just killed her in her car.

He jerked to a halt, faced her, looking insulted. "I didn't. That was Rodney. He was angry you'd ordered his firing, thought you didn't deserve your job. He hated you long before that though. I took care of him."

*Keep him talking*, she ordered herself. Because if he wasn't talking, he would be doing other things. She fought off a shudder. "Took care of him?"

"I killed him for you!"

Oh God, this man was completely nuts. "So you saved me from Rodney?" She swallowed down the bile as she asked the question.

His eyes went wild and manic. "*Exactly*. I knew you would understand. He was smart. Not as smart as me," he said smugly. "But he used different badges to maneuver his way around the system. He would have gotten caught even with his precautions, but I'd already put the security feeds on a loop."

"Why?"

"Because I needed the mobility around the office to watch you," he said simply.

Oh, God. *Do not show your revulsion*, she ordered herself. "Did you attack me at the hospital?"

"No. Never. I never wanted to hurt you. That's why Rodney had to die. I killed him for you. Don't you understand, I did that for you? I even mugged you when you were out with Geno. I thought... I thought you'd turn to me! I would have comforted you. I would have done anything you wanted." Spit flew out of his mouth as he raged.

She swallowed hard. "You never even acted as if you were interested in me."

"I did. I asked you out when I first started working there!" he snarled, his face reddening even more. She blinked, trying to remember, but she couldn't. He must have read her expression because his face scrunched up in rage again. "You don't even remember, do you? It was humiliating."

"I'm sorry," she whispered as fear snaked up her spine.

"You're going to be even sorrier for rejecting me." He crawled onto the bed, his breathing sawing in and out, his eyes wild—and that was when she noticed the big knife in his hands.

## CHAPTER TWENTY-SEVEN

Heart in his throat, Evan crept along the side of the exterior wall of the single-story house. Carefully, he peered into the window of the garage and saw the truck with the push bar. This was it.

It took all his restraint not to kick the door in or smash through a window, but he had to be smart.

He had to be quiet above all.

He'd parked a block away and raced here. The police were on their way but he wasn't waiting for them. Hell, Ollie could hear the sirens and kill—

No, he couldn't let his mind go there. He had to focus.

Considering what Ollie did for a living, Evan didn't want to risk getting caught on a security camera. He didn't see any on this side of the house so he wrapped his fist with his shirt and broke one of the garage windows as quietly as possible. No alarm sounded.

He got the window up and crawled through the opening. The door that led inside was locked and it took precious seconds to pick the lock.

Weapon up, he eased the door open and swept into what turned out to be a mudroom. A pair of boots was by the door as well as an umbrella on a hook. Two empty laundry baskets sat on a washing machine and the room smelled dusty, as if it hadn't been used in a while.

Pausing, he listened, waiting for an alarm. Nothing.

Panic swelled. What if she wasn't here? No, the truck was, and Ollie couldn't have gone far with her.

Weapon at the ready, Evan grasped the other handle and turned. Bracing for an attack, he swept into another room.

Living room. It was dark, save for a single lamp on a table by a plastic-covered couch.

Silently he moved through the house, looking for booby traps or cameras. Though at this point, if there were cameras, it was too late. He wasn't stopping.

At the sound of a muffled groan, his heart stuttered in his chest. Following the sound, he raced through the living room toward a hallway. Light spilled out from under a closed doorway.

He heard the groan again, then a muffled cry.

*Isla.* There was no time to wait, no time to be cautious.

Lifting his leg, he slammed his foot against the door. It splintered under the impact, cheap fiberboard flying everywhere as it busted against the wall.

What he saw would forever haunt him.

Isla was tied up on the bed, Ollie on top of her, cutting her clothes off with a hunting knife.

She let out a silent scream against the tape across her mouth, her eyes wide with terror.

Ollie turned, knife in hand. His eyes were wild, manic. He raised the knife high above Isla's chest, his intent clear.

Evan didn't think, didn't hesitate.

He pulled the trigger.

*Pop. Pop. Pop.*

Ollie jerked forward, crimson spreading out over the back of his yellow shirt as he slumped onto the bed.

Evan tucked his gun away as he raced toward the bed. Grabbing Ollie's body, he threw him on the ground, not bothering to check his pulse. The guy was dead or would be soon and Evan didn't give a shit about the monster.

He eased the tape off Isla's mouth and started cutting the ropes with his Swiss Army knife as she cried.

"You're safe now. I've got you," he said as he worked. "I've got you," he repeated, more for her or himself, he didn't know. And no one would ever hurt her again. He was going to spend the rest of his life trying to keep that vow.

Once she was free, sobs racked her body as he gathered her up in his arms. Her clothes were in tatters so he held her close as he lifted her up into his arms. Kicking the knife away from Ollie's still body, he stepped away from the bed.

"Did he act alone?" he asked, something he should have asked before.

"Yes. Just him," she managed to get out through hiccupping sobs.

Gathering her tight to his chest, he hurried out the way he'd come as she cried against his neck. In the garage, he opened the door and stepped out into the cool, night air as it rose above them.

Sirens sounded in the distance and he let out a sigh of relief.

"I'm going to set you on your feet so I can give you my shirt." He knew Isla enough that she wouldn't want anyone seeing her like this.

She nodded, tears streaking down her face as he quickly ripped his shirt over his head and slipped the tattered remains of her clothing off. His shirt was big and long enough to reach her mid-thigh. He belatedly realized she could see all of him—his ugly scarring—but he didn't give a shit. He was a fool. A damn fool for worrying about his scars.

Wanting to comfort her, he cupped her cheeks gently. "I need you to listen. Can you understand what I'm saying?" He was pretty sure she was in shock or going into it so he spoke slowly and softly.

"I'm listening," she whispered as the sirens grew louder.

"The cops are almost here. I called Duarte. They're definitely going to take both of us in. Probably separate us. They might take you to the hospital but they won't let me go. I'm calling my lawyer right now. Just tell the truth. Stick to the truth and we'll be fine. And know that as soon as I'm out of questioning, I will get you. I'm sorry but I know how these things work and they will definitely separate us." Something he hated with every fiber of his being, but he needed her to be prepared. To understand what was coming.

She nodded and leaned into him, wrapping her arms around him as she buried her face against his chest. "Evan," she whispered his name, all she could seem to get out.

Holding her tight with one hand, he quickly called his attorney and told him to meet him at the police station before disconnecting.

He'd done nothing wrong in killing Ollie to save Isla, but he still knew he would have to answer questions, and the State's Attorney would make a decision on whether or not to prosecute. He knew they wouldn't prosecute given the circumstances, but still, they would have to follow protocol to the letter. There was a dead body involved and he'd discharged a weapon. It was just the way things worked.

The only thing that mattered was that Isla was safe. If for some insane reason they decided to prosecute him, he didn't give a shit. He'd do it again a million times over to save her.

# CHAPTER TWENTY-EIGHT

I sla stood up from her hospital bed as the door opened and her mom rushed in. "When did you get here? How did you even know—"

"The police called me." Her mom hurried across the room in a flurry, her ankle-length dress swishing noisily before she pulled her into a bone-crushing hug. "Oh honey, I'm so glad you're okay, though I'm a little fuzzy on the details."

"I'm so glad you're here." She hugged her mom back tightly, fighting the onslaught of tears. She'd already had a breakdown after Evan had saved her and she'd barely been able to get through the police questioning. Thankfully they hadn't pushed too hard given her state, but she wanted to keep it together until she got home. "I'm really glad you're here," she repeated as her mom finally stepped back.

Her mom wiped tears from her eyes. "I've already spoken to your doctor, and you're free to go."

*Good.* She'd been planning to check herself out if they didn't let her. "I need to call Evan and we need to go see Geno Conti. He was admitted, and one of the nurses let me know that he's out of surgery." Thankfully it sounded as if he was going to come through it fine, but still, he'd been *shot*. "I can't believe that psycho shot him. Mom, I

know what the police told you, but...Ollie was be-
the bombing."

Her mom nodded, her jaw tightening even as tears
..ed her eyes. But she blinked them back before
straightening. "I've already spoken to the detective in
charge and he relayed what you told him. I'll get more
details later but it's my understanding that Ollie somehow blackmailed the bomber."

"Yes. At least that's what he told me."

Her mom stepped back and ran her hands up and
down Isla's arms as she inspected her like she was looking for unseen injuries. "Did that man...*hurt* you?"

Her skin crawled at the memory. "Yeah, but not like
you're asking. He was going to. And then Evan stopped
him. God, Evan. I need to call him now." She'd already
tried multiple times from the hospital phone, but it kept
going to voicemail. "I don't know if he's still down at the
police station, but—"

"I've already spoken to him. He's being let go and I
told him to come to my house. After we see Geno, I'm
taking you back home."

"I would like that a lot." The thought of going back to
her condo didn't hold any appeal, but going back to the
place she'd grown up? Even with all of its mixed memories, it was home. And she needed to feel safe again. She
was just glad that Evan was being let go and would be
meeting them there, because she needed to see him too.
Needed to hold him and know that he was okay.

He'd come for her, had saved her life. She had a feeling she was going to be having nightmares for a long

time about what had happened in that awful room, I
at the end of it, Evan had been there.

\* \* \*

Evan was desperate as he steered down Sophia
McDonald's driveway. He knew Isla was safe but he still
needed to see her. Needed to wrap his arms around her.
After the police had arrived, she'd been taken immediately to a hospital and they'd refused to let him go with
her, as he'd predicted. He understood that they had
needed to follow protocol, but it hadn't made things easier.

He threw his truck into park and was barely aware of
rushing up the walkway until the front door opened. So
he must have knocked.

To his surprise Sophia stood there and not her assistant, Rosa.

"She's sleeping right now so you can stop all that
banging." Stepping back, she let him in.

He hadn't even realized he'd been banging on the
door. His heart rate was jacked up as nerves punched
through him. "She's okay?" he demanded.

The last time he'd seen her she'd been crying in the
back of an ambulance, and he'd been unable to go to her.
He scrubbed a hand over his face. The image of her crying as they'd shut the doors ate away at him. If he could,
he would go back and kill Ollie all over again.

"She's okay. She's a tough cookie." Taking him off
guard, Sophia stepped forward and pulled him into a

He hugged her back as she said, "Thank you
my baby girl. I couldn't have survived losing

either," he rasped out. "For the record, I'm sorry
ay I treated her before, and I'm never going to
again. I'm in this for life."

ook was assessing as she stepped back. "I believe

van?" Isla stepped out into the foyer, wearing pa-
as he'd never seen before—navy blue pants and a
ong-sleeved thermal top with little unicorns on them.
Her auburn hair was down around her shoulders, her
eyes sleepy. His chest tightened at the sight of her.

"You shouldn't be out of bed." Her mom's tone was
worried.

"I thought I heard voices. Are you good? Did the police drop everything?" She hurried toward him in sock-
clad feet.

He gathered her close, something inside him easing
as he held her. "It's a clear case of self-defense. There
won't be any prosecution. Your mom is right though.
Let's get you back into bed."

Looking exhausted with dark rings under her eyes,
she simply nodded as he wrapped his arm around her
and walked with her to her bedroom. Her hair was
slightly damp and smelled of shampoo.

"I got here as soon as they let me."

"I'm glad. Stay, Evan." She looked up at him as he shut
the door behind them. "Please stay."

He couldn't believe she was even asking. "I'm not going anywhere." Gently, he guided her back to the rumpled sheets of her bed and slid in with her, but not before taking off the T-shirt the police had given him. Worry about his scars, his body, seemed like such a distant, unimportant thing after everything that had happened. She accepted him for who he was, period. He knew that.

She turned on her side, sliding her arm around him and burying her face against his chest. "Thank you...for what you did."

"Oh honey, don't thank me." He rested his chin on her head as she remained still against him, grateful to feel her warm and alive next to him. "I love you. I'd do anything for you."

"I love you too," she whispered. "God, I was so scared. I didn't know if anyone would come for me. I just... I didn't know how anyone would know."

He felt wetness on his chest as she quietly cried. "I'll always come for you." Always. He'd walk into hell itself for her.

Eventually all the tension in her body eased and she fell asleep while he held her close. He hadn't thought he was tired, but as soon as she fell asleep he dropped off too, his mind at peace since she was safe and in his arms.

# CHAPTER TWENTY-NINE

Isla startled awake, jerking up in bed, her heart racing after the nightmare she'd had. Thankfully it was just a dream and she was at her childhood home. *Safe.*

"You're okay," her mom said, making her turn.

Isla found her mom sitting in the rocking chair in the corner of the room, a well-worn paperback in hand that she quickly set aside. Sitting up, she pushed the covers off. "What time is it?"

"It's three in the afternoon on Saturday. You slept hard. Evan didn't want to leave your side but I convinced him to go take a shower in one of the guest rooms. I'm sure he'll be back here in a few minutes." Her mom got up and slid into bed next to her like she'd done when Isla was a child.

Despite all the issues she'd had with her mom, this was exactly where she wanted to be. Isla curled up against her, resting her head on her mom's shoulder.

"My sweet baby girl, I'm so glad you're okay." Her voice wobbled slightly. "We almost lost you."

"Evan saved me." She had a feeling she was going to need some therapy to come to terms with everything.

"How'd you sleep?"

"Good, but I feel like I need more of it." She might have slept a long time but she was still exhausted, as if she'd run a marathon. When she closed her eyes, she kept seeing Ollie's crazed face and that knife.

"You take all the time you need. Listen...I don't know if this is the right time to tell you, but I've gone to two AA meetings recently."

She shifted slightly. "Seriously?"

Her mom rubbed a gentle hand down her back. "Yes. I wasn't going to tell you until I'd been sober a month but...I'm trying," she whispered.

More tears sprang to Isla's eyes but she stayed where she was, curled up against her mom. "What brought this on?"

"One of my new bunco friends has been in AA for twenty years. She agreed to be my sponsor. I've tried over the years, you know. To get sober, I mean. Sometimes I'd be sober for a month or even six months. But I'd always go back." Exhaustion colored her mom's voice. "I probably shouldn't even be telling you, but I just wanted you to know."

Surprised, Isla sat up, leaning back against her pillows as she turned to face her mom. "I never knew that."

"I know. Your father did. And he always gave me chance after chance. I'm not sure why." Her eyes clouded over with tears for a moment.

"Because he loved you."

"Yes, he did." She patted her daughter's cheek gently. "And it's clear that Evan loves you. I know it's not my business, but I hope you give him a second chance. He deserves it."

"I know." He did deserve it. The man had screwed up, and yeah, it was a big deal. But he'd been trying to make things right ever since he'd come to his senses.

And he'd saved her life. If that wasn't a sign, she wasn't sure what was.

# CHAPTER THIRTY

*Five days later*

Isla stepped out onto the lanai, surprised to see Evan sitting with her mom, enjoying breakfast. He'd been staying here the last week, but had left late last night because he'd had some international work conference calls to make down at the office. She'd thought he might head back to his condo when he was done.

She'd completely stepped back from work since her attack and had let Madeleine take over for right now. She trusted the other woman and could admit that she wasn't ready to deal with the media storm or people in general anyway. Well, most people, because Evan's family—all of them except Ellis—and Jemma had been over a lot the last few days, bringing food and just keeping her company. So she'd been staying put at her mom's house and ignoring the news and anything related to what had happened. She was ready to step back fully, to let others take over the reins of her father's business even before she sold it.

Evan stood when he saw her, smiling that sweet, charming smile she felt all the way to her toes.

"How'd you sleep?" her mom asked. It was the first question she'd asked her every morning since her rescue.

244 | KATIE REUS

"Much better." Though the truth was, she would have slept better if Evan had stayed the whole night through. But she certainly wasn't going to tell him that and make him feel guilty. He had a job and a life and couldn't abandon it while she dealt with things. He'd been her shadow the last few days but that couldn't continue long-term.

"Are you ready for some coffee? Fruit? Eggs?" He was sort of hovering, looking nervous as he watched her.

The nervousness was a little weird given that they were officially and truly back together.

"If you two will excuse me, I have to go talk to Rosa about something." Her mom left, but not before giving Isla a kiss on the cheek as she passed.

"I'm actually not hungry right now," she said, leaning up on tiptoe to kiss him. She'd had another fitful sleep and didn't feel like eating or drinking anything.

Well, she could eat Evan up, but that was different. This morning he was dressed in a sharp business suit, looking as if he'd already conquered the world. Which he probably had.

Now she was glad that she'd pulled on a jersey wrap dress, deciding to actually put on something a little nicer than the yoga pants she'd been living in. She felt fresh and a little more human this morning, even with the bad dreams. She wasn't ready to go back to work and definitely not ready to face the world, but she felt better. And she would take the progress.

"Want to take a walk?"

"That sounds good." It was early enough that the sun was low in the sky and there was a nice breeze in the air.

She wanted to be outside, to take advantage since Florida weather could be fickle. Linking her arm through his, she leaned her head on his shoulder as they started along the little stone path that led around her mom's huge estate. "So how did your meeting go?"

"Good. Everything is in order, but I won't bore you with the details. I talked to Detective Duarte today too. The case is officially closed."

The tightness in her belly loosened the slightest fraction. "Good." That word seemed so simple for how she felt, but she was glad this nightmare was over. It seemed as if Ollie had taken an obsessive interest in her six months ago when his girlfriend had dumped him and left the country, moving to Europe with her now husband. She and Ollie's ex had a similar look, willowy and slender with auburn hair. At least that's what the police had gathered from digging into computers and other facets of his life. He'd been part of some horrible online forums with members who seemed to hate women in general so they'd been able to piece together a fairly good—if disgusting—picture of Ollie.

He'd somehow latched onto her and, using his insider's track with security in the building, had been watching her closely. His hacking had been the reason for the security glitches as the system tried to figure out what was wrong. He'd also been stealing from the company, which wasn't exactly a surprise since he had the moral capacity of a rock. He hadn't been lying about Rodney either.

246 | KATIE REUS

If Ollie hadn't hacked into the security, however, the rest of the team would have caught Rodney sneaking into her office and leaving that cookie—among other things. And it turned out that Logan did not have a gambling problem. Ollie had been planning to set him up for her murder. And now the police thought they might be able to link him to the deaths of some high-level escorts who had a similar look to Isla as well. Apparently when she'd hired Red Stone to do an audit of the security system it had spurred him into taking her. He'd been so damn worried they'd figure out what he'd done and that he would lose his chance to take her.

The guy was a grade A psychopath, and knowing all she did now—especially the fact that he'd gotten her father killed, and almost killed Evan—she was glad he was dead. It felt savage to even think that, but she wasn't sorry for it.

"Let's sit here." Evan guided her to the little bench in a private part of her mom's garden.

It was like a little fairyland back here, all bright, cheery and full of jasmine and lavender. Even though it was fall, flowers were still blooming, colorful and wild everywhere, a tropical paradise.

"How long do you think you want to stay at your mom's place?" His question was softly spoken and one she was pretty sure he'd been holding off on asking.

"It's been nice staying here. Peaceful. But I can't hide here forever. I was actually going to see what you thought about…"

"What?"

"Look, I'm just going to put it out there. I don't want to move back into my condo. You and I had planned to live together and I'm pretty sure we're on the same page now."

He kissed her, hard and fast, nearly startling her, but she leaned into it as his tongue teased against hers. He'd been so gentle with her the last few days and she hadn't realized how much she needed this from him. As usual, he had a knack for taking her breath away. All too soon he pulled back, his eyes fierce. "We are definitely on the same page. Move in with me. I don't want to spend another night without you. We were practically living together before anyway. It just wasn't official. So let's make it official. And if you don't like the condo, we can buy another place. A house. Wherever. I just want to live with you."

More tension inside her eased at his words. She wasn't even sure why she'd been nervous about asking him. "I want that too."

"Isla...I love you. I know I've said it, but I want to keep saying it. I've never stopped loving you and I'm not going to. You're my other half." In an unexpected, fluid movement, he slid off the bench and got down on one knee in front of her.

It took a moment for her brain to compute what he was doing as he pulled out a familiar-looking box. When he opened it she saw her engagement ring. She stared at him as he held the box out, and she was surprised to see his hand trembling.

"It's probably too soon. Every therapist in the world would say it was too soon. But I love you. There is no one else in the world for me. I want you beside me for the rest of my life."

"Is there a question in there?" she whispered.

His grin was slow and sexy as he pulled the ring out. "Marry me?"

She nodded, her throat tight with emotion. "Yes," she managed to rasp out as he slid the ring into place. *Yes, yes, yes.*

She didn't care if it was too soon. And she didn't think it was anyway. She'd almost died. Was definitely on the same page as him. There was no one else in the world who fit her like he did. Whether he asked now or months from now, the answer was going to be yes, so she wasn't going to delay the inevitable. She wasn't going to put a stop to something she wanted with every fiber of her being. Life was far too short. Something they both knew well.

"I love you," she said as she leaned forward and brushed her mouth over his.

He deepened the kiss until he was sitting on the bench and had pulled her into his lap.

"I think we need to get out of here now," he growled.

"Yes." She hadn't been ready for sex the last few days and it had felt weird, anyway, being at her parents' house. Now she was ready to get back to their home, to start their life. They'd been given a second chance and she was going to grab it with both hands. "Take me home, Evan."

"This came for you," Isla said as she strode into the kitchen—their kitchen. It felt kind of weird to think that after she'd had to come to terms with her and Evan not being a couple. But now they were engaged to be married as soon as humanly possible and she'd officially moved back into his condo. Their condo.

He glanced over from the stove where he was cooking something that smelled delicious. And he was shirtless, just like he'd been before the bombing, before everything. His scars were fading, but the puckered skin had a long way to go until the red was completely gone. Thankfully he was comfortable with her now, seeming to barely notice his scars when they were together. She was glad, because she wanted all of him.

"What is it?" he asked.

"I grabbed the mail on the way up. There's a postcard from Montana."

He took it from her, his eyebrows rising as he read aloud what was on it. "I think I found a way to make things right."

She'd already read it, but wasn't sure what it meant. "Who's it from and what does that mean?"

"Pretty sure it's from Ellis. It's his handwriting anyway."

She sucked in a breath at the mention of his brother, who'd gone on the run after being accused of murder. "You think he's found a way to clear his name?"

"I'm guessing that's what he means. At least I hope so. I just wish he'd reach out."

"Well, it kind of looks like he did."

"I mean in person. Or by phone. I miss his voice... I miss my brother." Evan let his wall down with her, let her see his agony at missing his brother.

She crossed the short distance and wrapped her arms around him, holding him close. "This postcard has to be a start, right? He's found a way to clear his name and we'll help him any way we can."

"We?"

She pinched his side gently. "Of course, *we*. He's my family now too."

"Thank you."

He didn't need to thank her, not for this. Before she could respond, he leaned down and kissed her, soft at first before deepening it. And before she knew it, he'd turned off the stove and lifted her into his arms.

Dinner was definitely going to have to wait.

Thank you for reading Bishop's Queen. If you'd like to stay in touch with Katie and be the first to learn about new releases, sign up for her newsletter at https://katiereus.com

## ACKNOWLEDGMENTS

As always, I owe a lot of thanks to Kaylea Cross, Sarah and Julia. Thank you guys for helping me whip this book into shape. To Jaycee, I'm grateful for another wonderful cover. For my readers, thank you guys for your wonderful reception of book one in this trilogy. I hope book two was all you hoped for! For my family, thank you for all your support. And of course I'm grateful to God for everything.

**Darkness Series**
Darkness Awakened
Taste of Darkness
Beyond the Darkness
Hunted by Darkness
Into the Darkness
Saved by Darkness
Guardian of Darkness
Sentinel of Darkness
A Very Dragon Christmas
Darkness Rising

**Deadly Ops Series**
Targeted
Bound to Danger
Chasing Danger (novella)
Shattered Duty
Edge of Danger
A Covert Affair

**Endgame Trilogy**
Bishop's Knight
Bishop's Queen
Bishop's Endgame

*Paranormal Romance*
Destined Mate
Protector's Mate
A Jaguar's Kiss
Tempting the Jaguar
Enemy Mine
Heart of the Jaguar

## ABOUT THE AUTHOR

Katie Reus is the *New York Times* and *USA Today* bestselling author of the Red Stone Security series, the Darkness series and the Deadly Ops series. She fell in love with romance at a young age thanks to books she pilfered from her mom's stash. Years later she loves reading romance almost as much as she loves writing it.

However, she didn't always know she wanted to be a writer. After changing majors many times, she finally graduated summa cum laude with a degree in psychology. Not long after that she discovered a new love. Writing. She now spends her days writing dark paranormal romance and sexy romantic suspense.

For more information on Katie please visit her website: https://katiereus.com

Made in the USA
San Bernardino,
CA